CONSTABLE ALONG THE LANE

A perfect feel-good read from one of
Britain's best-loved authors

Constable Nick Mystery Book 7

NICHOLAS RHEA

Revised edition 2020
Joffe Books, London
www.joffebooks.com

Cover credit: Colin Williamson
www.colinwilliamsonprints.com

**Join our mailing list and become one of 1,000s of
readers enjoying free Kindle crime thriller, detective,
mystery, and romance books and new releases.
Receive your first bargain book this month!**

ISBN 978-1-78931-406-9

CHAPTER 1

How shines your tower, the only one
Of that special site and stone!
EDMUND CHARLES BLUNDEN, 1896—1974

Among the unpaid benefits in the life of a village policeman is that of leisurely patrolling the beautiful lanes which pattern and serve our countryside. Every season has its delights and my patrols took many forms. Sometimes I toured the villages and hamlets in the section car, at other times I depended upon my official-issue small, noisy but reliable Francis Barnett motorcycle. But by far the most pleasant and rewarding way of performing my duty was to meander among the cottages and along the lanes on foot. The seasons did not matter — every day had its own charm, but this allowed precious time to see the sights, smell the perfumes and hear the sounds of England's living and ever-changing countryside. There were times when my slow pace made me feel part of the surrounding landscape.

By comparison, the car and motorcycle were speedy and functional as they presented the image of a busy police officer going about his vital work with the aid of modern technology. The latter was in the form of an official radio fitted to both the car and the motorcycle. The crackle of that radio, the zooming off into the unknown to go about some urgent mission, plus the polished livery of the police vehicles with the occasional flash of blue light or sound of a multi-tone horn, served to nurture an essential aura of efficiency and style.

Early morning patrols by car or motorcycle were generally spent in the eternal search for cups of tea, people to talk to and the occasional evidence of criminal activity of the rural kind. If I am to be honest, our missions were seldom urgent, unless executed in response to a traffic accident; the truth is that those pastoral wanderings enabled us to see a great deal of the changing landscape and the people who lived and worked there. The car, but more often the motorcycle, carried me through the hills and valleys, across the moors and dales, past ruined abbeys and crumbling castles and along the highways and byways, invariably on a route which had been prearranged by a nameless senior officer.

In fixing our routes, he would try to incorporate several villages and hamlets within, say, a three- or four-hour patrol, where we halted hourly in nominated villages. There we had to stand beside the telephone kiosk in case we were required. Someone in the office would ring us on those telephones if necessary. The fact that we were equipped with radios did not change that ancient routine because hourly points at telephone kiosks had been a feature of rural patrolling for generations. The system could not be abandoned simply because we now had radios! Senior police officers do tend to be belt-and-braces types, especially where their patrolling subordinates are concerned.

In my rural bobbying days, they liked to know what their village constables were doing at every moment of their working lives. It was an admirable method of stifling initiative but it also revealed their lack of confidence in themselves and a corresponding lack of trust in us. Nonetheless, the system did ensure that every tiny hamlet, as well as the more populated areas, received a regular visit from a uniformed officer, particularly at odd hours of day and night. As a piece of positive policing, they were valueless but they did keep our supervisory officers content in the belief that they had us just where they wanted us. And the public did see us going about our endless missions and probably wondered why we were passing at such peculiar times when nothing had happened.

But from my point of view, I did enjoy the early morning routes, as we called them, especially in the spring and summer, even if I had to drag myself out of bed at 5 a.m. at least once a week. But when the sun was shining, the birds were singing and the air was redolent with the scents of new blossom, it provided experiences I would not have missed for the world. I saw nature and the countryside at its beautiful best and the freshness of the morning made me glad to be alive and to be working in such amenable surroundings. To patrol with an accompaniment of the fabulous dawn chorus; to see young animals and birds enjoying their first taste of life and to hear the season's first cuckoo never ceased to thrill.

But even in such bucolic circumstances, it's nice to dodge the official system. As I started those routes from my hilltop police house at Aidensfield, I did so in the happy knowledge that there were several calling places on my patch. There I could enjoy a break from the routine or a spot of refreshment and human companionship. Farms and bakeries provided early morning buns and cups of tea which were most welcome during a tour of duty. In addition, the tiny police station at Ashfordly also provided sanctuary.

So far as Ashfordly Police Station was concerned, I had to be very careful; like all my rural colleagues, I had to enter without the resident sergeant hearing me, because if Sergeant Blaketon was woken by one of his tea-seeking constables, he would rapidly and effectively make his displeasure known and we would thereafter be denied that calling place.

For an erring constable, life would be hell for a short time thereafter, and so we all adopted a simple technique. We would park our motorbikes some distance away and walk to the police station. This silent approach was most effective.

After 6.30 a.m. however, the doors were open because that's when Polly, the station cleaner, arrived. Approaching sixty-five, she was iron-haired with grey eyes and the clean, fresh complexion of a countrywoman. She fussed over our little station as if it was her own immaculate home; she polished the furniture and brasswork; she cleaned out the fireplace; emptied waste-paper baskets and, if the cells had been occupied, she cleaned them and aired the blankets. And if Alwyn's chrysanthemums were in the cells, she would make sure they were tended.

Polly's strength lay in the fact that when one of the rural constables was performing an early morning route, she knew he was abroad because she could decipher the contents of the duty sheet. Knowing he'd love a cup of tea, she always had the kettle ready.

This little ritual meant that at some stage between 6.30 a.m. and 7.30 a.m. (when Sergeant Blaketon usually left his bed), Polly would put the kettle on and brew a pot of hot tea, as a result of which the early patrolling constable would pay a visit to the police station. There he would enjoy tea, biscuits and a chat with Polly.

If Sergeant Blaketon happened to wake early to try and catch us, Polly would hear him moving upstairs and would stand her mop in the front porch as a warning that Blaketon was likely to appear. This was the signal for us to head into the lanes of Ryedale and to the next kiosk on our agenda, thirsty but devoid of any slanderous criticism from our supervisory officer.

Sometimes, though, Sergeant Blaketon would surprise everyone by creeping downstairs in his slippers. To cope with that eventuality, we always carried some reports or papers which provided us with an excuse for being indoors. "I've just popped in with these papers, Sergeant," would be our excuse, at which he would retort, "Well, don't hang about here, stopping Polly from working and don't loiter when on duty!"

But by and large, those many little subterfuges worked to our advantage. The police office at Ashfordly became a regular haven of refuge, one which was particularly welcome during winter patrols. During those dark and chilly mornings, when our fingers, toes and ears were frozen, Polly always had a blazing fire and her splendid cups of tea to warm us. But through every spring, summer, autumn and winter for years, Polly had been there with her fire, her cups of tea, her awareness of the sergeant's movements and, in times of need, her warning mop at the door.

Then a crisis came to Ashfordly Police Station.

Polly retired.

We made a fuss over her departure and had a farewell party in one of the local pubs. Sergeant Blaketon made a nice speech and presented her with a portable radio we had bought for her.

That we missed Polly was never in doubt, but for a few idyllic days afterwards, we did honestly believe we could encourage any new cleaner to be as thoughtful and accommodating as Polly. But Sergeant Blaketon had quietly made his own decision about the kind of person who would be suitable for the appointment and we were to learn to our sorrow that his ideas did not correspond with ours.

My first encounter with the new cleaner came that April. The appointment had been made only days before and upon my first tour of duty afterwards, I was performing one of those early morning routes. I had started at 5.30 a.m. from my police house at Aidensfield, and had made my first point at Elsinby at 6.05 a.m. with my second at Briggsby at 6.35 a.m. As Ashfordly lay only a five-minute ride from Briggsby, there was time for a quick visit to the police station before my 7.05 a.m. liaison with another in my allotted chain of telephone kiosks.

If my colleagues had done their work efficiently, the new cleaner would have lit the fire; the kettle would be boiling and it would be known that a lonely, patrolling constable was in need of tea, warmth and amiable companionship.

As I made my lonely vigil outside Briggsby's kiosk, I wallowed in anticipation of a hot cup of tea. The early spring morning was, in Yorkshire terms, "nobbut a fresh 'un", the real meaning of that description being that the morning was extremely cold. Indeed it was, for April can produce some very chilly northern mornings; it can also produce some memorable April showers, and in both achievements it excelled itself that morning.

As I stood shivering beside my motorcycle with the cheerful singing birds for companionship, I wondered momentarily whether I was in the right job. After all, other folks were still in bed or had warm cars to carry them about their work. As I pondered upon the unfairness of a constable's life, the heavens opened.

In a matter of minutes, the beautiful blue morning sky had been obliterated by a mass of swiftly moving black clouds, some with delightful silvery edges. As they succeeded in shutting out the rising sun, they opened their taps. Huge dollops of heavy rain lashed the earth from that sombre ceiling and in seconds, the roads and fields were awash with urgently rushing water and dancing raindrops. In seconds, brown rivulets were gushing from the fields and roaring along the lanes.

In my heavy motorcycling gear, I was reasonably prepared for most kinds of weather, but on this occasion, water ran down my neck and into my boots as the pounding rain bounced off my helmet and battered my face which was already sore from the effects of a chill morning breeze. The downpour persisted for several minutes, then the monstrous black clouds moved to a new venue upon their journey of misery and the sun came out.

Brilliant and warm, it caused the roads to dry a little and the birds to resume their singing. As I climbed aboard my motorbike, little clouds of steam began to rise from the tarmac, and as I kicked the bike into life, I wondered if the rain had waterlogged the electrical essentials. But it started without any trouble and I chugged over the hills to enjoy the dramatic vista as I dropped into Ashfordly. As I motored sedately into the valley, I could see the beautiful effects of that awesome shower — the glistening pools in the fields as they reflected the morning sun; the patches of rising mist as the water evaporated in the bright coolness of the day; the sheer greenery of the panorama before me and the freshness of the new spring colours. It was as if the landscape had had its morning bath.

But I was cold as the pervading dampness soaked into my clothes beneath my motorcycle suit. The one salvation was that a few minutes drying out before the lovely fire in Ashfordly Police Station would cure that problem. On the final run-in, I drove through some running rivulets, some lingering pools of muddy residue which the downpour had produced. Very soon, my boots, legs and machine were spattered with mud.

When I arrived at the police station, therefore, I was soaked outside with the mud and residue of the roads, and inside my clothing with rain that had flowed down my neck. I coasted the final few yards to avoid arousing Sergeant Blaketon and having parked the little motorbike, I switched off the radio. With visions of hot tea before me, I prepared to enter the warm office.

I was surprised when a powerful voice bellowed "Out!" It was a voice I did not recognise.

I stood for a moment in the porch, stamping my feet on the doormat and I must admit that I did not immediately connect the voice with my arrival. I continued to stamp in an effort to shake off the surplus water and then the inner door opened.

I was confronted by a short, thick-set fellow with a bull-like neck and cropped hair. It was still black but shaven so close that it looked like a well-worn black lead brush. Two piercing grey eyes stared at me from the depths of the heavy, pale features of a man dressed in a long, brown dustcoat. He'd be in his middle fifties, I guessed, and was only some 5 feet 5 inches tall. But he looked and behaved like a bulldog.

"Out!" he ordered. "Get out of here!"

I stood my ground, still shaking off the after-effects of that shower. "Who are you?" I demanded. "You can't tell me to get out. I'm not even in yet!"

"And you're not coming in, not like that. I've cleaned the floor, I'm not having muck dropped and paddled all over. Taken me hours to get it something like it has, so clear off."

"Who are you?" I asked again, having stopped shaking off the water as he stood in the centre of the doorway to effectively block my entry. It would require a strong physical action to shift him, I reckoned.

"Forster. Jack Forster, I'm the new caretaker."

"Caretaker? Cleaner, you mean."

"Caretaker," he affirmed. "I takes care of this police station, so I'm a caretaker. Now, if you want to come in, you'll have to go into the garage and get rid of that mucky suit. Leave it there to dry off and make sure your feet are clean. I'm not having you lot messing up my floors. So you and your mates can all get that into your heads right from the start. I don't clean floors so that folks can muck 'em up again."

"I'm soaked, I want to dry myself in front of the fire," I said. I wanted to see if there was any compassion in that squat, powerful frame.

There wasn't.

"Not here," he continued to block the doorway. "Yon fire's not lit. I'm not lighting that fire while I'm working, it makes me too hot when I'm polishing. It's laid, but I'm not lighting it today. So you've no need to come in, have you?"

"I've got some official business to conduct," I said. "Telephone calls to make, reports to read. I'm on duty," and I stepped up towards the door, but he stood his ground, determined.

"Then take them mucky clothes off," he said. "Otherwise, I'll get Sergeant Blaketon to issue an order saying no motor-bike suits allowed in here. I'm not having my floors messed up, no way. Look at you mud, water, muck everywhere!"

I was in a momentary dilemma. He had no right to bar an officer from his own police station, but I was acutely aware that if I physically moved him aside, he might lodge a complaint. He seemed the kind of person who might claim he'd been assaulted by a policeman. Time and time again in police circles, we met cleaners and similar operatives who used their mundane tasks as a source of petty power over others; cooks, cleaners, domestics, car washers there was always one who lusted after power and who liked to exercise his or her own brand of dominion over others. This man was of that breed, and the fellow was here, in Ashfordly, blocking my route into the office.

If I ignored his demands, he would, without any shadow of doubt, run to Sergeant Blaketon. He would then take great delight in banning us from using the office as a refuge and tea-room. This meant that I had the future welfare of myself and my colleagues to rapidly consider as I stood dripping before this little Hitler. The options flashed through my mind as I watered the floor of the outer porch. Already, I had created a distinctive pool of mud.

But as I swiftly considered the alternatives, I concluded that, under no circumstances, must a trumped-up cleaner be allowed to succeed in banning me or my colleagues from the station. That fact must be established immediately.

I was tempted to use bad language to express my views but realised this could also be used as ammunition when this fellow made his inevitable complaint to Sergeant Blaketon.

"Mr Forster, by standing there, you are obstructing a police officer in the execution of his duty," I said with as much pomposity as I could muster and thrust him aside as I pushed into the office. I don't think that accusation would have convinced a court, but my action took him by surprise. Any threat of greater authority, I knew, would compel him to retreat. He did, but he was not finished.

"You'll regret this, you'll be disciplined!" he began to shout as he backed into the office. "I'll have Sergeant Blaketon informed of this, so help me!"

Once inside, I made a great show of ringing up Divisional Headquarters, reading circulars, checking my in-tray, reading notices and generally doing all the routine chores which were expected during a formal visit of this kind. And all the time I dripped mud and water along my circuitous route across Forster's floor. I felt some guilt but justified my conduct because of his uncompromising attitude. He followed me around, red-faced and angry, fuming at the mess I was leaving in my wake, and threatening all manner of actions from my superior officers. I decided not to stay for tea. The atmosphere was not conducive to a relaxing visit, and the fire was unlit anyway. It was laid out with regimental accuracy with the fire-irons arranged in sequence upon the hearth and the coal heaped neatly upon the paper and sticks. Those portions of the clean floor gleamed like polished silver. I was reminded of my days in the RAF, doing National Service, when we polished the floors of our billets to such a standard that no one dare walk on them. We moved around by sliding on little mats made from old blankets, one to each foot.

That ensured the floor was always polished and saved us lots of time on Bull Night. Now, this floor was heading that way. But, having messed it severely, I left. I found a welcoming bakery where I warmed myself as I enjoyed a nice bun and a mug of hot tea, and soon I was glowing amid the scents of newly baked bread and cakes.

Later, I discovered that Forster had complained to Sergeant Blaketon. To give the sergeant some credit, he had not spoken to me about the affair of the muddy visit which perhaps revealed something of his disdain for the nature of the grumble, but he did resort to his normal tactic — he displayed a typed instruction on the police station notice-board. Each of us had to read and initial it.

Sergeant Blaketon was prone to issuing typed instructions through the medium of the station notice-board. We learned that the degree of his anger was reflected in the method of typing — a notice produced in black lower-case type was routine. This might embrace matters like holiday dates, special duty commitments and so on. A black notice in upper-case type was more important — that could include warnings not to use the office telephone for private calls or to make sure our monthly returns were submitted on time.

A notice typed in red was rather more serious. If it was in lower-case red type, it was of considerable import — such as 'Members will refrain from revving up their motorcycles outside the station at 2 a.m.' or 'Members *will* repeat *will* study all Force Orders and *will* repeat *will* initial each copy when it has been perused.'

We were never instructed to 'read' papers and documents — always, we had to *peruse* them, and we were always classified as 'members' in Sergeant Blaketon's vocabulary. I never did find out of what we were members.

But a very important notice was always typed in red upper-case letters. For example, 'MEMBERS WILL STUDY THE ACCOMPANYING PHOTOGRAPH OF THE CHIEF CONSTABLE AND WILL ACKNOWLEDGE HIM IN THE STREET BY SALUTING' or 'MEMBERS WILL *NOT* REPEAT *NOT* USE OFFICIAL VEHICLES FOR COLLECTING GROCERIES OR FISH AND CHIPS.'

After my first meeting with Jack Forster, therefore, an instruction did appear on the station notice-board. In lower-case red type, it said, "Members will take every care to keep the police office clean and tidy at all times and should not enter in soiled motorcycle protective clothing unless unavoidable owing to the exigencies of duty."

The 'exigencies of duty' was a marvellous phrase for making exceptions to most rules, and when this notice appeared, the story of my meeting with Forster became widely known. So did the reason for the appearance of this order, and from that time forward, we discovered more of his tactics. He objected to smokers putting cigarette-ends in ashtrays; he disliked tea or coffee cups being left unwashed; he objected to paper containing crumbs of food being placed in the waste-bins; he wanted all lights switched off when the office was empty; he objected to out-of-date posters being left on the notice-board and apple cores on the mantelshelf. In fact, he objected to everything and everyone. He seemed to have a passion for cutting official expenditure which probably explained his unwillingness to light the fire, his passion for switching off lights and his theory that much of the paperwork in the office was not necessary. I think he based this judgement upon the amount of wastepaper which accumulated in the waste-bins. The outcome of his arrival was that the office *did* remain clean and tidy, chiefly because we rarely went in. There was no longer any pleasure in visiting our little section headquarters and the result was that the lanes around Ashfordly were very regularly patrolled. We made very frequent visits to establishments like hotels and bakeries which offered warmth and occasional refreshment, and we also made use of each other's homes.

In one sense, the social life of our happy little section was enhanced because we saw more of each other and of each other's families, but it was clear that Sergeant Blaketon was growing concerned about our unwillingness to make regular visits to the office. To circulate our paperwork, we tended to rely upon his visits to us, rather than our visits to him. To counter this, he compiled an instruction, in red lower-case type, about the matter.

It read, 'Rural members *will* repeat *will* visit the Sectional Office at Ashfordly at least once during each tour of duty. It is essential that all members keep up to date with correspondence, local procedures, new legislation, Force orders and internal instructions. This instruction is effective immediately.'

And we all had to initial it and comply. Thereafter, we made these token visits to collect our mail and to obey Sergeant Blaketon's order, although most of us managed to make our visits when Jack Forster, whom we nicknamed Jack Frost because of his chilly nature, had completed his daily stint. He worked from 6.30 a.m. until 9.30 a.m. each morning consequently avoidance was not difficult, except when working an early route.

But overall, the effect of his presence could not be ignored. We moved around the clean, tidy office as if it was a showroom of some kind, hardly daring to touch the furniture or leave footprints on the floor. We cursed Jack for his cussedness, and we cursed Sergeant Blaketon for engaging him. I must admit that I often wondered whether poor old Blaketon had really foreseen what the outcome of Forster's appointment would be.

Some of us did try discreetly to frustrate or annoy Jack. We did paddle upon his floors; we did leave wastepaper lying about; we did spill tea or coffee from our flasks and we did make the office look as if it was a place of work and not a disused museum.

But the real punishment for Jack arrived late one night; it was something that could never have been planned and it was doubly pleasing because it could be logged under that wonderful heading 'Exigencies of duty'. I was pleased too, because I was the officer involved. I felt that some kind of poetic justice had descended upon Jack Frost.

It so happened that I was not working one of those motorcycle routes but was performing a full tour of night duty in Ashfordly. A complete week of night duty came around every six months or so, when we worked from 10 p.m. until 6 a.m. the following morning.

I was patrolling on foot in the outskirts of Ashfordly. It was 1.30 a.m. and I was looking forward to my meal break which was scheduled for 2 a.m. I would take that break in Ashfordly Police Station, careful not to dirty the place because of Jack's ferocious responses.

During patrols of that nature, we kept our eyes open for villains and villainy of every kind, from drunken drivers to car thieves, from burglars to cattle thieves, from runaways to tearaways. So when I saw a small, rusty Morris pick-up inching slowly along Brantsford Back Lane without any lights, my suspicions were immediately aroused. It was moving jerkily and rather noisily towards me, and so I decided to investigate.

My first job was to halt it so I stepped into the lane and flashed my powerful torch at the vehicle, waving it up and down in the manner then used to halt motor vehicles.

Always wary that vehicles of this condition might not have brakes, it was unwise to stand right in front of them. The procedure was to keep clear as they came to a halt, and then move in to continue the investigation. But there were no problems as the slow-moving pick-up came to a halt with my torch shining into the driving-seat.

The driver, a thin-faced individual with thick, dirty hair, looked pale and ill and he awaited me with a suggestion of resignation on his face. I opened the driver's door, removed the keys from the ignition switch and said, as all policemen do, "Now then, what's going on here?"

"Summat's gone wrong wi' t'electrics," he said in a hoarse whisper. "Sorry, Officer. Ah know Ah shouldn't have drove, but Ah had ti git 'ome . . ."

At that point, there was a tremendous rumpus in the rear and some heavy object caused the pick-up to rock and sway, so I hurried to the back. A massive pig, a Large White sow, was struggling to climb over the tailboard, and as I reached the back, she half-tumbled, half-climbed from the vehicle into the road. Fortunately, she did not gallop off; judging by her massive size she would have difficulty even in walking, so she stood close to the vehicle, snuffling around the rear wheels. I saw that she had a rope attached to one leg but there was no way I could get her back into that vehicle. He must have had a ramp of some kind for her to climb up.

It was then that the contents of a crime circular of some weeks ago echoed in the recesses of my mind. There'd been regular thefts of livestock in the area over a period of months and some livestock owners had reported seeing a small, darkened vehicle leaving the scene late at night . . .

I grabbed the end of the rope and clung to it, then said, "This pig. Is it yours?"

The fellow in the pick-up made a non-committal response. I followed with a request for his name and address, and asked where he had obtained the pig. He produced more non-committal and indecipherable replies.

"Come along, out you get," I said. "Leave the van here. We'll talk about this at the police station."

"No, Officer, Ah can explain . . ."

"In the police station!" I had made up my mind to question this fellow in the security of the station. The van was in a quiet lane and was parked on the verge where it was not a danger to other traffic. After noting its make, size, colour and registration number, I discovered it was not taxed either. There'd be a catalogue of traffic offences here, so I seized the driver's arm with one hand and kept the pig's rope in the other. "Police station!" I said as I guided man and pig towards Jack Forster's shining palace.

The fellow shuffled along, sometimes groaning and sometimes uttering words which I did not understand. I jollied the huge sow along the road by slapping her ample back from time to time as she waddled contentedly through the streets. She was clearly domesticated and seemed unflustered by this turn of events.

Sometimes, she would stop for a snuffle in the hedge bottoms, but she was no real trouble. Her companion was no trouble either as he walked, with some support from me, towards the station.

Sergeant Blaketon was having a day off, so I knew I must not arouse him. I told my captive to hang on to the pig's rope, which he did, as I unlocked the door of the office. As I switched on the light, the big sow hurried inside, dragging the man with her, and I followed, closing and locking the door for security.

"Has thoo arrested me?" was the man's first question as the lock went home.

"Yes," I said, for I did not want him to leave. Had I said, "No, you are just helping with enquiries," he might have decided not to assist with the many enquiries I must make.

"What for?" he asked.

"Suspicion of stealing that pig," I said. "So where did you get it?"

He sighed. "Aye, all right, Ah took it. From a sty over Brantsford way. Don't know whose. If that truck o' mine hadn't brokken . . ."

I cautioned him and wrote his admission in my notebook, then obtained his name and address, age and occupation. He was Cecil Matthews of 56 Roselands Road, Ashfordly, forty-three years old and a general dealer. Having checked this, I said, "Right, I'll have to get a sergeant to see you. So it's the cells for you and for that animal!"

I searched him, listed his belongings and placed him in Cell No 1, and then, by putting on the light of Cell No 2, persuaded the waddling, grunting sow to go in there. She seemed to like places that were well-illuminated because she went straight in. It was the Female Cell anyway, which I felt was appropriate, although it was very bare now that it did not house Alwyn Foxton's chrysanthemums. He was replenishing his stock, I think. Having locked up my two prisoners, I rang Eltering Police to contact the duty sergeant.

It was now after 2 a.m. I told my story and he said he'd come immediately. I made a cup of tea and took some in for my prisoner, then settled down for my break. I had sandwiches, a piece of cake, an apple and a cup of tea, then Sergeant Bairstow arrived.

"Now, Nicholas old son. Where's the prisoner?"

"In the cells," I said. "He's admitted pinching the pig. I got a voluntary out of him. He can't remember whose it is, but it's from somewhere near Brantsford."

"Ah! A nice easy case then? Good for you. Right, I'll have words with him, then I'll charge him and bail him out from six o'clock. You stay here in the office until six, and then send him home. I'll bail him to Eltering Court for next Friday."

"Right, Sergeant."

"And the pig? Where is it?"

"In No 2 cell, Sergeant," I said. "There was nowhere else . . ."

"The van? Why not leave it where it was?" he cried.

"It got out," I explained. "And there's no way to get it back in. It's docile enough . . ."

"Right, the minute somebody comes on duty at Brantsford, get them to find out whose it is, and have the bloody thing collected. We can't keep pigs in the cells . . ."

"Yes, Sergeant."

And so the official procedures for prosecuting Cecil Matthews were put into action. Sergeant Bairstow dealt with him kindly but firmly, and then we placed him back in the cell until six o'clock. Sergeant Bairstow departed about three o'clock, leaving me in the office until my relief came on duty at six.

Each half-hour I peeped into the prisoner's cell to check that he was safe, but around four-thirty, he started to produce some ghastly noises. He began calling for help. I went in, wary that it might be a trick of some kind, but it was clear that the man was ill. Beads of perspiration stood out on his forehead and his face was a dull, pasty green colour; he was holding his stomach and was doubled up with pain.

I rushed to the telephone and dialled for Doctor Williams for I had no wish to have a man die while in my custody. After explaining the problem, he said he would come immediately, in spite of the hour. When he arrived only minutes later, a dour, heavy man, I showed him into the cell; he recognised Cecil and after a brief examination, said in his lilting Welsh voice, "stomach trouble, Constable, it is."

"Is it serious?" I was genuinely worried.

"Not so that it will kill him, you know, but he'll be very ill for a while. Gastric troubles, of long standing they are. Now, I have something in my bag which might be of help . . . leave him to me . . ."

I left the cell, glad to be away from the suffering man, but I then became aware of more awful noises, this time from the adjoining cell. Screeching, heavy snufflings and grunt-ings, painful cries. I hurried to the door, but was unable to open it. When I slid back the inspection hatch, I could see that the huge sow was lying against the door, holding it shut as she uttered the most pained and piercing of cries. It sounded like many pigs in distress.

I was in two minds whether to ask the doctor for advice but felt he might be offended; even so, her cries were agonising and so I decided to call the vet. Not giving me time to explain the somewhat unusual story, he said he would come immediately.

When he arrived, he made an initial examination through the inspection hatch and smiled.

"She's farrowing, giving birth," he said. "Soon, the place will be full of little pigs . . ."

I groaned. "How many?" was all I could ask.

"Ten or twelve perhaps. She's a Large White, so she'll have a lot. Large Whites always do, Constable. Some achieve twenty a farrow. Yours is she?"

I explained in detail how she came to be here, and he laughed. "Well, there's a bonus for the loser. He's lost one and will gain many. Now, if you don't mind, I'll hang on until she's produced them all, just in case there are complications. She'll roll clear of that door sooner or later, maybe to have a drink from that loo in the corner of the cell."

"Will you have a cup of tea?" I offered him.

"Love one," he said. "Three sugars."

I went off to make a cup of tea, and when I returned, I found Doctor Williams having a hearty laugh with the vet, a man called Harvey. We sat and discussed the patients, Doctor Williams saying that Cecil's stomach would result in him being sick all over the cell along with some uncontrollable diarrhoea, and the condition would persist until his gastric trouble had eased. Mr Harvey said the pig would make a mess too, what with giving birth and exercising her bowels . . .

And as I sat there, I wondered what Jack Forster would make of it all when he arrived at half past six. But I was off duty at six. I decided not to wash the cups either.

CHAPTER 2

When I was at home, I was in a better place
But travellers must be content.
WILLIAM SHAKESPEARE, 1564—1616

Having been compelled to spend more time patrolling the lanes around Aidensfield and Ashfordly, it was inevitable that I should become more deeply acquainted with Arnold Merryweather's rattling old buses. In their faded purple and cream livery, the pair of them were a familiar sight in Ryedale. They provided a vital means of transport and an equally valuable method of communication for many of the villagers. Those without cars relied upon Arnold's buses to carry them to work or to the shops or merely on visits to relatives and friends; it was impossible to envisage a contented rural life without the service that Arnold provided.

His buses were never off the road, a fact which meant that on several occasions, I had to speak to Arnold about the condition of his vehicles. In his rustic and carefree way, he managed to ignore the laws which governed the operation of passenger vehicles. He seemed to think that the laws which applied to large companies and city transport did not apply to his little business.

He would use the aged buses as delivery vehicles and would carry parcels, goods and even livestock to market; I've even known him use a bus as a breakdown vehicle. Because they were always in use, their maintenance became somewhat suspect. In addition, his willingness to help others often led to him flouting or even breaking the law. Never did I prosecute him, although I found it necessary to constantly remind him of his statutory responsibilities. And, in his own way, he did try.

"Aye, Mr Rhea, Ah'll see to it," he would say. "One o' these days, Ah'll get it fixed" or "Ah'll get Hannah to make sure it doesn't happen again."

But he seldom did get it fixed, whatever it was, and he relied on Hannah, his huge conductress, to exercise her own judgement over the events which occurred on board the service bus.

Miss Hannah Pybus, with her loud voice, masculine appearance and authoritative manner, kept order and, in her own way, helped Arnold's business to thrive. Unattractive though she was, there was always a hint of romance between Hannah and her boss. Thick-set Arnold, with his mop of ginger hair now greying slightly as he progressed towards his sixties, seemed an ideal partner for the tall and equally thick-set Hannah. Her heavily freckled face and mop of sandy hair complemented his features and even if she did walk along his aisles with the swaying gait of a sailor, we all knew there was some attraction between them.

But their romance never blossomed. I think this was because Arnold spent all his working days either behind the wheel or in the depot in Ashfordly effecting repairs. In addition, his limited leisure time was spent in the Brewers Arms telling Irish bus jokes and drinking Guinness.

His only contact with Hannah was on board his bus. After work, she would mount her trusty cycle to ride home to Thackerston. Occasionally if the weather was bad, Arnold would place her cycle in the bus and take her home, but he never went in. He never took her to a restaurant, the theatre or cinema, or even to the local pubs. One reason was that his only mode of transport was his bus! Hannah would say, "If you think you're taking me to the pictures in that, you've another think coming!" The result was that not once, to my knowledge, did Arnold enjoy a social outing with the formidable Hannah.

For those who have not been introduced to Arnold's bus service through my *Constable Around the Village*, he operated along the picturesque lanes and through the pretty villages between Ashfordly and York. Each day, one of his groaning coaches, furnished with wooden seats bolted on iron frames would leave at 7.30 a.m. and weave its slow way through Briggsby, Aidensfield, Elsinby and beyond until it arrived in York.

It made a return journey, and then a second trip from Ashfordly to York, making a final return trip at 5.15 p.m. On Fridays, Arnold's other bus made a special run to Galtreford because it was market day and lots of rural folk regarded that as a day out.

During these runs, Arnold carried the village workers into the city where he did bits of shopping and ran errands for those who could not make the journey. He collected eggs *en route*, delivered laundry, and performed a whole series of useful deeds, many of which probably infringed the various laws which governed the use of public service vehicles.

Arnold's helpfulness is illustrated in an incident in which he came to the aid of the constabulary. The same incident also highlights the importance of a village policeman's knowledge of his patch and the things that occur on it. In this case, that knowledge involved the route, timing, halting places and general *modus operandi* of Arnold's bus service.

Just after eight o'clock one Wednesday morning, I received a frantic telephone call from Abraham Godwin, an animal feeds salesman who lived in Aidensfield.

"Mr Rhea," he panted into the mouthpiece, "my car's been stolen, just now. Less than a minute ago . . ."

The urgency of his voice propelled me into action, although I had just got out of bed, having worked until two o'clock that same morning. I was not feeling on top of the world. In less urgent circumstances, I would have adopted the well-proven procedures of having details of the car immediately circulated to all our patrols. I'd have then recorded the details in a statement before filing the event in the criminal records and stats files. It would rest upon some other distant police officer to locate the vehicle when eventually it was abandoned.

But as the thief had just struck, it didn't make sense to follow the normal procedures. With only a minute's start, it might be possible to catch the villain.

I'm sure that thought was also in Godwin's mind.

"Which way did it go?" I asked.

"Towards Elsinby. The thief's dumped another in my drive, Mr Rhea, an old Ford," he panted.

"Right, what's your car number?" I asked.

"DVN 656C," he said. "A red Hillman . . . you know it."

"I do, but my colleagues don't. So," I said, "I'll come to see you soon, but I've work to do right now if we're to catch him."

And I slammed down the telephone. I knew it was utterly futile dressing in my motorcycle gear to give chase. That would take several minutes. In the meantime, the stolen car, especially if driven by a thief, would be racing away and I would never catch it. It was time for immediate, albeit unorthodox, action.

I looked at my watch. It was five minutes past eight and I knew that Arnold's bus would be trundling towards York. If I was right about the habits of an opportunist car thief, he would also be heading for the city, either to vanish there or to steal another car to continue his journey. The fact he'd dumped one in Godwin's drive suggested he was hitching lifts through the countryside by stealing a succession of available cars.

I looked at my map. I tried to recall the day I'd once used Arnold's bus on its circuitous journey into York and reckoned his bus would, at any moment, be calling at Hollin Heights Farm.

He called regularly to collect a load of eggs and actually took the bus into the farmyard to do so. I rang Jim Harker, the farmer, and he answered.

"It's PC Rhea," I said. "Has Arnold's bus got to your spot yet?"

"Just coming doon oor lane, Mr Rhea."

"It's urgent that I speak to him," I tried to stress the urgency of this call, but I knew old Jim Harker could not rush. That was something he found impossible.

"Ah'll tell him," said Jim, and I heard the handset being placed on a hard surface. I could only wait. But surprisingly, only a minute or so passed before someone picked it up.

"Merryweather," said the voice.

"Arnold," the relief must have been evident in my voice. "It's PC Rhea. I need help."

"Fire away, Mr Rhea, Ah've time to listen while they're loading t' eggs."

Once before, I'd advised Arnold not to carry loads of eggs on his bus because it was illegal but there was no time to worry about that. I explained that Godwin had just had his car stolen and that it seemed to be heading towards York. I began to describe it, but Arnold said, "I know it, Mr Rhea, that red Hillman."

"I wondered if you could halt it, Arnold," I said. "I know there might be a risk, but if . . ."

"If that car comes up behind me, Mr Rhea, Ah'll stop him. Then Ah'll call you," and the phone was replaced.

It was a long shot, but it might work. I now made the necessary formal circulation of the stolen car's particulars by ringing our Control Room and Divisional Headquarters. I arranged for the CID to visit Godwin's home to examine and fingerprint the dumped vehicle and executed all the formalities that were associated with a reported crime.

Having done this, I hurried down to Godwin's house, explaining to Mary that if Arnold rang, she should contact me there. To save time, I drove down in my own private car. Godwin, extremely upset at the audacity of the thief, was still in a state of anxiety, but I suggested he take me into the kitchen where I asked his wife to brew some coffee. The performance of a mundane domestic chore often removes a good deal of tension; besides, I hadn't had my breakfast.

Godwin explained that after starting his car, he had driven it on to his forecourt where he had left the engine running to warm thoroughly. After locking the garage, he'd gone into the house to collect his briefcase and papers. While doing that, a strange car had entered his drive and driven onto the lawn. A slim youth in his early twenties and dressed in a pale green sweater and jeans, had then jumped out and had got straight into the waiting Hillman. Then he'd driven off at speed towards Elsinby and York. For sheer cheek and opportunism, this theft was almost unique.

It took me a while to complete the necessary crime report forms. I required the engine and chassis numbers in addition to the more obvious details, and explained it was necessary if the car was altered or broken up; parts of it might still be identifiable and for that reason, our C.10 branch, the stolen car experts, would need those kind of details.

I made a rapid examination of the dumped and ancient Ford, noted its number on Godwin's phone, rang the details to Control Room. Efforts would be made to trace its owner and the source of the theft, if indeed it had been stolen. All this took about three-quarters of an hour, and then the telephone rang. It was Mary, slightly breathless.

"Arnold's stopped that car," she said. "He rang from Woodland Hall, that's about a mile the other side of Craydale. He's got your thief; he's at the entrance to the Hall. He says can you go straight away, so he isn't too late into York?"

Godwin beamed with pleasure at the news, but I was worried about the state of his car. Thieves have no respect for the vehicles they use so carelessly and so it was with some apprehension that I asked Godwin if he would come with me and drive his own car home. He agreed.

Twenty minutes later we arrived to be confronted by the results of Arnold's remarkable bus-driving skill. The thief had been trapped too, so my arrest was easy.

Afterwards, I learned how Arnold had contrived this. While driving his bus and its assortment of passengers out of Craydale, he'd noticed the red Hillman approaching from behind. When the speeding car was level with the rear of his bus and overtaking it, Arnold had eased over to his offside, keeping pace with the car. The car, now with a very anxious driver at the wheel, had been forced to move over and as the vehicles sped along, Arnold's mighty bus had moved still further to its wrong side. In that way, it had literally forced the stolen Hillman off the road and into a shallow ditch.

It had been trapped on one side by the high drystone walls of Woodland Hall and on the other by the bus. The driver had become a prisoner, and the Hillman had suffered some minor damage to the offside front mudguard.

Afterwards, I discovered that Arnold had given his passengers a running commentary to explain his odd behaviour, but as his bus had drawn to a halt beside the trapped car, a young passenger had leapt out. Quickly, he had placed two large stones from the Hall's wall behind the wheels of the car, very effectively preventing it from reversing to freedom.

The bus's position across the road meant that traffic could pass by, although some did stop to enquire if they could be of assistance at the 'accident' but Arnold had declined. And so, thanks to Arnold, we caught a car thief.

I submitted a report to the Chief Constable about Arnold's actions. In gratitude Arnold was presented with a 'thank you' letter and a helmet badge mounted on an oak plaque. The press publicised the tale too, which gave him and his coach service some useful publicity, but this was minor praise in comparison with the hero status he was awarded by the local people and regular customers.

On another occasion, Arnold used his bus as an ambulance. I happened to be using the bus at the time. It was a Tuesday.

Arnold had eased his groaning old coach to a halt out-side the gate of Ridding Farm on the moors above Elsinby, where Aud Mrs Owens boarded it for her weekly trip to York market. Inevitably, Arnold and his passengers had to wait as the diminutive figure of Mrs Owens pottered up the long track laden with baskets.

That Tuesday, however, we noticed two figures making their slow and painful progress towards the bus. One was Mrs Owens and the other was her husband, Kenneth, who seldom appeared in public. His life was spent almost entirely on the farm; he had no car and no wish to see what lay beyond the boundaries of his spread. He led a life of self-sufficiency and seclusion.

As the couple approached Arnold's bus, it was evident that Kenneth was hobbling painfully.

I saw he was using a home-made crutch. It was simply a broom upturned, the head tucked under his right armpit and the shaft supporting his limping progress. His right leg, which wore a Wellington boot, was held awkwardly aloft in a kind of sling which had been created by tying a length of rope about the sole and ankle of the Wellington, then up and around his neck and shoulder. It kept his foot off the ground.

Kenneth's age was a matter of debate. He would be well over fifty, probably nicely into his sixties. Today, he wore some soiled corduroy trousers which bore evidence of many years of work and milking cows, and a rough, grey denim jacket, hereabouts called a kytle. A battered, flat cap deco-rated with a patch of cow hairs sat low upon his head and concealed most of his thin, weary face. The cow hairs were from his habit of resting his head on the flanks of the cows as he milked them.

His wife gave little support as poor old Kenneth made his slow, difficult way towards the bus. I was about to offer my help, but Mrs Owens anticipated this by calling, "Leave him be! He'll manage best on his own." Kenneth had a very difficult job manoeuvring himself up the steps into the coach, but with some help from Arnold and Hannah, and some cursing from his little wife, he made it and hopped into a seat. There he sank onto the wooden framework with an audible sigh of relief.

"And what's up wi' thoo, Kenneth?" asked Arnold as he slammed the bus into gear and began to guide it away.

"'E fell off an haystack," said Mrs Owens. "'E reckons 'e's brokken 'is leg. 'E should 'ave been watching what 'e was doing, that's what Ah say."

"Where are you taking him then?" It was Hannah's turn now as she hovered with her ticket-machine.

"'Ospital," was the reply.

"He can't walk from the bus station . . ." said Hannah.

"Nay, so you can tak 'im, it's only down a few side streets," she said. "Tak him on t' way in," she shouted at Arnold. "Leave him there. Ah'll see to t' milking and t' hens tonight."

Hannah looked at Arnold who was now in the driving-seat with his back to this little drama, but he simply said, "Aye, right-ho."

"So that'll be one return to York and back, and one to York only, for 'im," Mrs Owens ordered her tickets.

"Are you leaving him?" Hannah asked.

"Might as well," said Mrs Owens. "'E's nobbut a nuisance about the spot like this, huffing and sighing from morning 'til night, and Ah shall 'ave his hens ti feed and eggs to collect, then there's t' cows to muck out and milk . . .'e's as well off in 'ospital oot o' my road."

The subject of this discussion sat and said nothing as he gazed out of the window of Arnold's coach, his injured leg sticking into the aisle and his broom standing like a sentinel as he clung to it.

"Do you think he's broken his leg?" Hannah asked as she spun the handle of her ticket-machine.

"Aye, Ah reckon so," said Mrs Owens. "There was a mighty crack when 'e landed and his foot wobbled a bit. So Ah made 'im keeps 'is welly on, and then 'e couldn't walk on it cos his foot end went all floppy. After a day or two like that, we reckoned it was brokken. So Ah thowt we'd better get him seen to."

"When did it happen?" asked Hannah aghast.

"Thursday or Friday last week it would be. Ah've not 'ad a day's work out of him since, so Ah thowt Ah'd better tak 'im to 'ospital."

We overheard this curious exchange, but the placid Arnold simply drove on and collected more people along the route. In York, he diverted his bus from its journey and drove through some side streets until his bus full of people arrived at the Casualty Department of York City Hospital.

There, a repeat performance occurred as Mrs Owens, with help from several passengers, including Arnold, Hannah and myself, manipulated Kenneth and his brush off the bus. Once he was established on his feet outside, Mrs Owens pointed to a sign which announced, 'Casualty Department'.

"In there," she ordered Kenneth and got back on to the bus.

"Aren't you staying?" asked Hannah.

"Ah am not!" said the redoubtable lady. "'E's old enough to fend for 'imself and Ah've no time to fuss over a thing like that. Ah've got work to do in town. So come on, Arnold, let's be off," and she made her way to a seat.

Arnold hesitated for a few moments to make sure poor old Kenneth completed the short journey, but a nurse discovered him and eased his final yards into the building. Arnold then continued his journey.

On his first return trip, with Mrs Owens still somewhere in York, Arnold did make a second detour and personally called at the hospital to enquire about poor old Kenneth. He learned he had suffered a broken leg and that he would be allowed home when the doctor was satisfied the bone was healing and that the plaster cast was performing its function.

When Mrs Owens caught the bus on its second return run, she said, "Ah'll write 'em a note, Arnold, to see 'ow 'e's getting on, and when 'e's fit to come 'ome, mebbe you'll call and pick 'im up?"

"Right," said Arnold, not wishing to cause a flutter in the Owens' household by saying an ambulance would bring home the injured farmer.

Kenneth was brought home in due course and I found him hobbling about the premises with his pot leg as he fed the pigs and mucked out the cows.

He seemed quite content and said very little about his sojourn into city life. I realised that country folk like Kenneth and his wife were so self-reliant that they rarely ever asked anyone for help. If they wanted something doing, they did it themselves; their method of coping with Kenneth's broken leg was an example of that independence.

Arnold's bus service, however, called at another market once a week; this time on Fridays at the small market town of Galtreford. Arnold's second coach was utilised, with a relief driver as a rule.

I heard that when this bus travelled via Galtreford, there was a good deal of wheeling, dealing, buying and selling on board before the bus actually arrived. By studying the Public Service Vehicles (Conduct of Drivers, Conductors and Passengers) Regulations 1936, I learned it was illegal to beg, sell or offer for sale any article in the vehicle . . .

But, in rural areas, one closes one's eyes to a great deal, and really, I felt, this problem was not really mine. It could be argued that the enforcement of such rules was really the responsibility of the Traffic Commissioners, not the police.

So the minor infringements continued and they helped everyone aboard to feel content and happy. In fact, a trip to Galtreford market on Arnold's bus seemed to be a very jovial and happy affair.

Judging by the accounts which came to my notice, it was more of a party than a domestic outing or a bus trip. Songs were sung, for example, and drinks were handed around, albeit never to the driver when he was behind the wheel.

My very discreet enquiries led me to believe that a trip to market was a very sociable occasion which included community singing. This was led by two Aidensfield characters nicknamed Bill and Ben. In their late forties, they were inseparable and had been pals since their schooldays. They went everywhere together. Bachelors with no regular means of financial support, they went to Galtreford market every Friday.

Their real names were Arthur Grieves and Bernard Kingston; Arthur was 'Bill' and Bernard was 'Ben'. Each lived in a small rented cottage and undertook casual work in the area. They found employment on farms at potato picking time, harvest time and hay time; they took jobs on building sites, or washed windows — in fact, they would do anything anywhere for a small fee. They always worked together and it was their unhampered lifestyle that allowed them the freedom to go to market each Friday.

Arthur (Bill) was the elder by a few months and had lived in Aidensfield since birth. His mother, widowed in her twenties, had reared him but had died before I was posted to this beat. He was a dour character who said very little, and whose main interests appeared to be darts and dominoes at the Brewers Arms.

A stocky man, he had a square, weathered face with skin as tough as leather and thinning hair which encircled a tanned bald patch. In his mode of dress, he always appeared smart because he constantly wore a dark suit, a white shirt, a dark tie and black shoes, but closer examination would show that the suit was a little threadbare, the shirt could have done with washing and ironing while the tie bore evidence of several pub snacks and spilled beer. But from a distance, he looked fine.

Ben was more casual; taller than his friend by perhaps three inches, he was lean and angular, with a good head of dark, curly hair and a loping gait. Always untidy, his clothes generally seemed too wide or too long; sometimes he wore a grey suit, sometimes a pleasing sports jacket and flannels and occasionally, he would appear in casual wear such as jeans or a bright-squared shirt which made him look like a Canadian lumberjack.

Ben was rarely seen without a smile on his face; he always appeared to be happy with the world, and as he lived with his aged parents, he never had to worry about cooking his own meals or washing his own clothes.

All that kind of chore was done for him, and it was perhaps the influence of his mother which explained the size of his clothes. Maybe she still treated him as a growing boy who required clothes just a fraction too large so he could grow into them. I think she failed to realise he had matured. Like Bill, he spent a lot of his time in the Brewers Arms playing darts and dominoes.

Close as their bachelor friendship was, there was never a suggestion there was anything sinister or unsavoury in their behaviour, and no one even considered theirs was a homosexual relationship. It wasn't; they were two heterosexual men who loved a good time and who, in reality, had never grown up. Theirs was a life of casual ease with no responsibilities.

This eternally juvenile aspect of their existence had led to their outings at Galtreford market; ever since leaving school, they had made the weekly trip on Arnold's bus. Their mission was to wander around the market and then adjourn to one or other of the local pubs to sample the ale, play darts or dominoes and meet some of their acquaintances, especially those of the female sex.

When Bill and Ben got among the women, there would be banter and chatter, but nothing else; certainly no dates and no real courtships arose from these carefree meetings.

On the return journey these lads, as everyone called them in spite of their age, would lead the community singing on Arnold's bus. The more I heard about this outing, the more I thought I'd like to experience a trip to Galtreford market. I did not want to catch Arnold by identifying possible breaches of the many bus laws, but felt I'd like to experience the in-bus entertainment which seemed to cheer all those who travelled that route. I knew that singing on a bus was only illegal if it annoyed the passengers, and was sure this did not — how could it annoy if everyone joined in?

My opportunity came one Friday when I was having a day off duty. It was my long weekend. I had Friday, Saturday and Sunday off duty, a welcome sequence which came around once every seven weeks. On this date, it coincided with Mary's turn to have the local children's play-group at our house.

Several mums with tiny tots took turns in hosting a play-group; it allowed some of those harassed young ladies to take time off from their children, to enjoy a short shopping spree or to have their hair done and relax in other ways. Even though our four youngsters, aged between one and five, would make a class of their own, we both knew it was beneficial for them to mix with others of their age before starting primary school. So we joined that lively group.

On that Friday, it was made plain that if I remained at home, I'd be in the way. Because Mary might need the car to ferry home some of the visiting children, I felt the occasion presented me with an ideal opportunity to disappear by jumping onto Arnold's bus and experiencing the delights of Galtreford market.

And so, as I stood at Aidensfield bus stop at half past nine that morning, I was joined by Bill and Ben. As we waited, no one said a word and eventually others joined the little queue, including a large brown and white spaniel.

Eventually, Ben looked at me, his curiosity getting the better of him. He asked, "Gahin ti market then, Mr Rhea?"

"Yes," I said. "I've heard a lot about this outing, so I thought I'd come along."

"Then stick wiv us, Mr Rhea, we'll show you what's what, me and my mate. Do you play dominoes? We could do with a third hand."

"You're on," I said as Arnold's bus came into view. The little queue clambered aboard and from the outset, it was evident that Bill and Ben had their own seat. The spaniel pushed its way through the queue and slid beneath one of the other seats from where it eyed everyone, almost as if it expected to be ejected. But it wasn't.

Bill and Ben's seat was the first one inside the door, a prime position because it allowed Ben to pass comments about everyone who entered and, if necessary, to lend a helping hand to any aged person. As there was no conductress on this bus, (Hannah had travelled into York on the other one), their help was appreciated, even when spiced with bawdy remarks.

Ben's running commentary included remarks like "Howway, Mrs Preston, we can't hang about all day just 'cos thoo's gitten arthritis" or "If thoo taks onny longer gittin in, Elsie, this bus'll run oot o' petrol," or "Now then, Phyllis, leaving t' old man again, are we? Ah'll bet 'e's chuffed about that. 'E'll have that little milkmaid in ti mak 'is coffee this morning, mark my words!"

It was all part of the ongoing entertainment and Ben held forth with his chatty line of banter at each stop. The driver was one of Arnold's pool of part-timers and he bore the chatter in silence as he accepted the fares and guided the old bus towards Galtreford. It pulled into the market-place, halted with a groan of brakes, and everyone, including the spaniel, spilled out on to the cobbles to go their separate ways. It was just ten-thirty.

"Now then, Mr Rhea," said Ben, as I waited for their next move. "What's thy plans for today?"

"I have no set plans," I said. "I think I'll just have a look around, and then think about something to eat."

"Right," said Ben, who appeared to be spokesman for both. "Then thoo'll have a game o' dominoes with us, eh? In t' King's Head. We allus 'ave a mooch about till twelvish, and then settle in for t' day with dominoes. There's sandwiches, pork pies, pickled eggs and crisps in t' King's Head. We need a third hand, today. Thoo'll be there, eh?"

"Right," I said, and off they went, with the spaniel trailing behind.

I wandered around the colourful open-air stalls, listening to the banter of the traders and looking at second-hand books, antiques, furniture, crockery and all the other regular offerings of this busy little market. I enjoyed a coffee in one of the pubs which turned its bar into a coffee shop on market day mornings, and in no time, the town hall clock was striking twelve.

Somewhat apprehensively, I entered the King's Head, a fine-looking coaching inn just off the market-place, and spotted Bill and Ben seated at a table with the domino box already before them. Four pints stood beside it, and the spaniel lay beneath the table, apparently asleep.

"Yan o' them's yours." At my approach, Ben indicated the beers with a wave of his hand. "Flossie'll be here in a minute."

"Play this game much, then, Mr Rhea?" asked Bill, eyeing the box of dominoes as he spoke.

I shook my head. "Not a lot, we used to play at our training-school, or during break-times when we were on nights."

"Then you do know a bit about it. We play fives and threes, threepence a knock," Ben informed me.

"Fine," I said.

"And it's Nick, isn't it?" Then he leaned across and whispered, "We shan't let on thoo's a bobby, so thoo's among friends!"

"Thanks," I said, with genuine appreciation. It would be nice, being away from my own patch and being anonymous for a while, but I did wonder who Flossie would be. Then a heavily made-up woman arrived and sat down, sipped from one of the pints, and said, "Who's your friend, lads?"

"Nick," said Ben. "Pal of ours."

"Hello Nick," she said, and took a heavy draught. "Right, highest for off."

Bill upturned the box and spread the dominoes face down upon the table and he selected a six four. He had to play first. I was still wondering about Flossie who could have been any age between thirty and forty-five.

She was a brassy woman with a husky voice and very heavy make-up which was adorned with rich, red lipstick and nail varnish. But to this day, I don't know who she was or where she came from, or what she did for a living. But she could drink pints of beer with the best of the men, and I was to learn that she could play dominoes too.

As the game progressed, each of us bought at least one round of pints, and then we had a kitty to take us up to bus time. In between, we had sandwiches, pickled eggs and a pork pie each, which we shared with the spaniel, and the afternoon vanished in a haze of clicking dominoes and coins, shouts of delight, lots of spots totalling five or three or multiples thereof, and several pints of strong Yorkshire ale. Because, on market days, the pubs are open all day, we drank quite a lot.

I think I lost about six shillings and ninepence in all, but it was a very entertaining and relaxing way of spending a day. We all said farewell to Flossie, and at five-thirty returned to the bus stop, with the spaniel at our heels.

"We enjoyed that, Mr Rhea, thoo'll etti come again," said Ben.

"It'll be a long time before I get another Friday off," I managed to say. "But when I do, I'll come along. Thanks for inviting me to join your game."

"Flossie'd die if she knew you were a bobby," laughed Ben. "But she's good fun."

"Where's she from?" I asked.

"No idea," he said. "No idea."

And then the bus pulled in.

"If thoo hadn't bought all them taties and carrots, Mrs Baxter, thoo'd git onto this bus a bit faster," once more Ben launched into his commentary. "By, Mrs Harrison, Ah'll bet thoo's spent all this week's wages on that there kettle, and I happen to know there's nowt wrang wi' that awd 'un o' yours. Ah'll bet thoo reckons yon's a bargain. But what's your Fred gahin ti say? He nivver likes spending a penny . . . he's as tight as a duck's . . ."

Bill and Ben settled on their special seat, the spaniel slid beneath another and I occupied one, midway along the aisle. Then, as the old bus creaked away from the market, the singing started.

Led by Ben and a woman whom I did not know, it seemed that the entire complement of passengers joined in a happy programme of real sing-along songs like 'Mother Kelly's Doorstep', 'Ilkley Moor Bah't 'At', 'Maybe It's Because I'm a Londoner', 'Blaydon Races', 'Shine on Harvest Moon' and many more of that popular range. Bill and Ben produced bottles of beer from their pockets and so did several of the other passengers, women included, and a party atmosphere was rapidly generated.

The spaniel joined in by howling as some of the notes reached a high pitch, and I reckoned my own awful voice would not be condemned. So I joined in the noise too.

We would be around half-way home, when the bus eased to a halt in Partington. As it began to brake, Bill stood up and Ben clambered down the steps.

He jumped out as the bus halted, and so did Bill; the spaniel followed and so, because I now considered myself a member of their party, I did likewise. Others followed and said their cheery goodbyes, and the bus pulled away. We watched it leave as it echoed to the sound of happy singing; by now, the Merryweather Coaches Mobile Choir were well into 'Home, Home on the Range'. As it vanished around the corner *en route* to Aidensfield and Ashfordly, Bill, Ben, myself and the dog stood on the side of the road in silence. No one said a word. I have no idea how long we remained there in our little group, but I wondered if this was part of their market day ritual.

At length, I said, "Well, what now?"

Ben looked at Bill.

"Thoo got off," he said. "Why?"

"Ah didn't," countered Bill. "Ah just stood up to find my handkerchief. Thoo was t' one ti get off. Ah just followed."

"Ah thought thoo was getting off!"

"And Ah thought thoo was getting off."

"And I thought you were both getting off," I added.

The dog wagged its tail.

"Thoo was getting ready to get off!" snapped Ben.

"Nowt o' t'sooart," retorted Bill. "Ah just stood up to dig deep for my handkerchief, then thoo jumped off."

"Ah just jumped off because Ah thought thoo was gahin ti jump off . . ."

And so we stood there like three stupid Charlies, the bus now weaving its ponderous way through the distant lanes as the spaniel looked at us for guidance.

"It's a long walk back to Aidensfield, Mr Rhea," said Bill slowly, reverting to the formal mode of address now that our day was drawing to a close.

The walk home was about six miles, many furlongs of which were steep rising hills, but there was no alternative. How on earth we came to be here still seemed something of a mystery, but we started our long walk. The spaniel seemed to be enjoying this part of the day, for it frolicked in the hedgerows and along the floral verges of the long, winding lane.

"At least your dog's happy about it," I said to Ben as we got into our stride.

"It's not my dog, Mr Rhea," said Ben.

"Nor mine," added Bill.

"Well, it isn't mine," I felt I had to clarify that point. "Whose is it?"

Ben shrugged his shoulders. "No idea," he said. "But he's a grand little chap, reet good company. He comes wiv us ivvery Friday on that bus, follows us aroond t' market and then 'as a pork pie in t' pub. He likes yon pie and comes home on t'bus as well. He nivver pays a fare, 'cos nobody claims him, but Aud Arnold doesn't mind."

I could have inspected the spaniel's collar to determine the identity of his owner, but he was some distance ahead of us now, sniffing and fussing about the roadside vegetation. To be honest, there seemed no point in worrying about his owner — clearly, this dog was his own master, just like Bill and Ben, and he would go home in his own good time. They were three of a kind, carefree and content, with no respon-sibilities and no one to answer to. They went where they pleased; they did as they liked, and thoroughly enjoyed their method of existence.

I began to wonder whether I was envious of them as we strode out of Pattington. But once away from the cottages, Bill, Ben and I were subjected to the effects of the beer and desperately found ourselves having to attend to the needs of nature. We found a tall and sheltering hawthorn hedge, climbed over a five-bar gate into a field and stood behind that hedge like three sentinels as we watered the undergrowth to the accompanying sounds of intense relief. The spaniel joined us by cocking his leg against the gatepost.

Thus satisfied, we renewed our walk home, and had walked but half a mile when it started to rain. Instead of complaining or attempting to shelter, the happy pair began to sing 'April Showers' in the style of Al Jolson. The dog howled as they reached the higher notes and the rain intensified with every passing minute.

I was pleased no one knew me, for we must have seemed a strange quartet of men and beast. But I enjoyed walking along with this strange, happy-go-lucky trio of market-attenders; perhaps I did feel just a hint of jealousy over their carefree way of life.

As I contemplated their mode of existence, and as the increasingly heavy rain saturated my clothes and hair, I began to wonder what Mary would think when she realised I hadn't come home on the bus. A meal would be ready and she would be tired after hosting all those children, so I pondered upon her reaction when eventually I did walk into the house, weary, beery and wet.

Explanations would not be easy but I was pleased I didn't have to make my excuses to Sergeant Blaketon. I was reminded of an old piece of Yorkshire wisdom which goes, "Being late home from t' market often spoils a good bargain."

I lengthened my stride and joined the singing of 'April Showers'.

CHAPTER 3

When other lips and other hearts
Their tales of love shall tell.
ALFRED BUNN, 1796—1860

To those who have never been, North Yorkshire's image is seldom that of a land of sylvan beauty. They don't think of it as being graced by charming villages full of thatched cottages and peaceful ponds. But North Yorkshire's Ryedale, reclining on the southern edge of the North York Moors, can shatter those illusions, if indeed they lurk in the mind. For Ryedale is a valley of thatched cottages, peaceful inns and village ponds. There are charming woodland glades, ruined castles and abbeys, quiet streams and a countryside so gentle that it would be more in keeping with the south or the west of England.

One of the most photographed of England's thatched cottages is to be found here; it graces many a box of chocolates and country calendar. There are thatched inns too many of the villages boast interesting collections of thatched homes. Some are remote and some are positioned at the side of our main roads. Some have been modernized and some have had their thatch removed, while several are the old-fashioned cruck houses.

Most are single-storied and contain oak beams which are dark with age. They derive from the early long-houses of the dales, being built with little architectural skill, but with the essentials of rural life in mind. Quite often, the family lived at one end and their livestock at the other, but these lowly homes were functional and cheap both to construct and maintain.

Cruck houses, many of which still stand, were constructed from early in medieval times until late in the seventeenth century. Pairs of oak trees were used, each pair being shorn of their branches until a tall, straight trunk remained. These were positioned with the thick portion on the ground, and the tips were then drawn together and linked with a 'ridge tree' to form a letter A. When standing upright, one or two spars were fixed to them so that the 'A' shape had two or even three crosspieces.

Several of these 'A' shapes were used, each erected some five yards from the other, and they formed the framework of the cottage. They were linked lengthwise to one another by more beams and spars. Stone walls, a flagstone floor and a thatched roof completed the building, and many of these stand today.

When I arrived at Aidensfield to occupy the hilltop police house with its lovely views of the valley, I found great delight in locating these delightful cottages. At one time, I considered making a register of them, purely for my own interest, but somehow, never found the time. Perhaps this interest in old houses coincided with a sudden interest in buying and renovating ancient country cottages. People everywhere wanted to buy them and occupy them, and there was a ready market for all kinds of ancient piles.

Wealthy people from the cities bought all manner of hovels and spent much time and lots of money 'doing them up'. Some of the results were horrific, but it is fair to say that many were tastefully restored and brought back to life when, without this surge of interest, they might have been left to fall into total ruin.

Perhaps rural folk did not appreciate the architectural or historic significance of these little homes. They allowed them to be sold off, seldom making a bid to buy them. For them, the houses were often "That awd spot up t'rooad that's tummling doon and leeaks like a coo shed".

As I toured the lanes of Ryedale, therefore, I became aware of all the thatched cottages in their various locations and in their various stages of repair or disrepair. From time to time, I saw our local thatcher at work — we called him a theeaker — and marvelled at his casual skills. Sometimes the cottages would be completely gutted and rebuilt, with all their ancient oak interior woodwork and flooring being removed and replaced with modern fittings.

But occasionally, someone would come along and buy a remote thatched cottage, then proceed to restore it in its original form, albeit with modern benefits such as damp-proofing, up-to-date plumbing, central heating and electricity. When done properly, such a house could be a delight, a real gem.

It was during my patrols along the lesser known byways around Aidensfield that I discovered Coltsfoot Cottage, a pretty country home if ever there was one. Tucked behind a tall, unkempt hawthorn hedge and almost hidden among a paddock thick with tall rose bay willow herbs, it had a thatched roof, whitewashed walls and tiny Yorkshire sliding windows. These were, and indeed still are, a feature of some moorland and Ryedale cottages.

Owned by one of the local estates, it had for years been occupied by an elderly man who paid the tiniest of rents and who therefore lived in a rather primitive manner. His toilet was an earth closet; he had no hot water and no electricity and the floors were sandstone flags. The estate had offered to implement a full modernization scheme but old Cedric had declined.

Having lived in the house since birth, he had no wish to change either it or his way of life. Dark, damp and neglected, it was a tumbledown old house and was known to date to the seventeenth century. But the interior was lovely; dark oak beams, an inglenook, tiny cosy rooms and a position of almost total seclusion gave it the status of a dream cottage. It was the kind of house that the country cottage-seekers of that time were desperately hunting, and was probably more attractive because it was so very ripe for modernization.

From the quiet lane which passed the front gate, it appeared to be unoccupied and derelict, although there was a patch of garden which produced hollyhocks, delphiniums and several varieties of rose. Some of these climbed the walls and smothered the thatched porch with colour in the summer, mingling so beautifully with the honeysuckle.

When Cedric died, the estate decided that it would be too expensive to bring the cottage up to contemporary standards. The subsequent rents would never justify the expense and so it was placed on the market. And even as the estate agent's 'For Sale' signs were being erected, a wealthy insurance broker from London chanced to be passing.

With commendable speed and decisiveness he bought it; the price being very low due to its lamentable condition. But, like so many townspeople of the time, his great wish was to own a picturesque and isolated cottage wherein he could live a life of rural bliss far from the pressures of his high-flying career. It was a place he could 'do up'; it needed thousands of pounds and many man-hours spending upon it, but the new owner of Coltsfoot Cottage was prepared to do all that. He wanted the perfect hideaway and he had found it.

In my role as the village policeman, I had to be aware of events on my patch, and so I kept a discreet eye on the empty cottage.

I did not want it to be vandalised or occupied by unauthorised visitors such as squatters who might come across it and establish a commune there. But within weeks of the purchase, the new owner began to make his impact. He came every weekend and sometimes during the week; he did a lot of the work himself, although he did employ contractors for the specialised tasks. The theeaker came to re-thatch the roof;

a plumber came to install hot and cold water, a bathroom, shower and central heating while the electrician wired the house for lights and power.

A damp-course was installed; the garden was cleared; the walls were re-pointed and whitewashed and the wood-work was either varnished or painted. The exterior rubbish was cleared with the assistance of a JCB, and a drive and parking area constructed to accommodate his Rover and her MGB. This was laid with gravel which crunched when any-one walked across it, and then a small conservatory was added at the rear, partly as a draught-proofing scheme and partly to grow flowers and cacti.

Within a year, Coltsfoot Cottage had been trans-formed. Happily, roses still climbed up the white walls and trailed across the porch; but now, with its new roof of clean thatch and sparkling exterior, it was the ideal dream cottage. Modern, clean but incredibly beautiful, I would have loved to have been the owner, but such things were not for consta-bles. This man had money, and he knew how to use it.

During his weekend visits, I learned his name was James Patrington; once or twice as I patrolled past his gate on my little Francis Barnett, I would stop for a chat, ostensibly to pass the time of day and to make him aware that I was keep-ing an eye on his premises. Frequently, I found him in the garden dressed in a pair of old grey trousers, a holey brown sweater and Wellingtons. Sometimes, his wife was there too and one day they invited me in for a coffee.

They were a handsome, friendly couple; he was in his mid-forties and a shade less than six feet tall. Stockily built, he was balding and had once had a head of thick, black curly hair, evidence of which lingered about his neck and curled over his collar. Round-faced with dark, intelligent eyes, he smoked a heavy pipe, which never seemed to leave him, and told me he was a partner in a firm of city insurance brokers.

His wife, Lucy, would be in her late thirties and was almost as tall as her husband; slim and elegant, she had dark hair too, and this was showing signs of premature greying, something she did not try to hide and which therefore made her most attractive. She had very slender hands, I noticed, the kind one would expect in a piano player and her peach-complexioned face always bore a pleasant smile.

I was to learn that she ran a fashion shop in Chelsea and that its demands did not permit her to come to Coltsfoot Cottage every weekend. James, however, always seemed to be there from late on a Friday evening until late on a Sunday evening. I knew that he worshipped the cottage and he asked me to keep an eye upon it during his absence. This I was happy to do. I was supplied with both his business and home address, and his telephone number at both places in case of problems.

"Come and see my cacti," he invited one Saturday afternoon when I called. He was alone and led me into the conservatory at the rear where I saw hundreds of tiny plant pots. All were neatly labelled with obscure names and some plants bore incredibly beautiful flowers. "I grow these for fun, I suppose," he said. "I sell some, but I reckon that I've every known variety here and at my other home . . ."

And so I became on good terms with the Patringtons. I cannot claim friendship, however; the relationship was that of the village bobby and those who lived on his patch, a friendly albeit business-like acquaintanceship. But both of them always made me welcome and sometimes, I felt, when James was alone, he was glad of someone to talk to. Gradually, he did make his own friends in the area, people of the same professional class to which he belonged, and I would see him *en route* to the local inns or restaurants, or perhaps heading for a cocktail party or drinks gathering at one of the homes in the area.

Lucy, when she came, did not often leave the cottage. Sometimes, she drove up from London with James and sometimes, if she had to return early, she would drive up alone in her red MGB. Clearly, her own commercial interests kept her very busy and when she did come to Coltsfoot Cottage, she wished for nothing more than a quiet weekend before the blazing log fire in its oak-beamed inglenook, and perhaps a pleasant dinner with James at one of our splendid local inns or restaurants.

They came and they went, not interfering in the village activities, but simply enjoying the unhurried pace and solitude offered by Coltsfoot Cottage. Incomers though they were, they had rescued the old house from destruction and decay, for I'm sure that no local person could or would have raised the capital necessary to buy and renovate it.

Once the Patringtons were established, I saw less of them; every so often, though, I would receive a telephone call from James advising me that he would not be at Coltsfoot that coming weekend and asking if I would keep an eye on the cottage during my patrols. It would be about two years after he had bought the cottage, that their pretty little home hit the headlines of the national newspapers. It happened like this.

High on the hills behind Aidensfield lies the Yorkshire and North of England Sailplane Club, one of the busy gliding clubs of this area. Gliding is very popular from here because the lofty moors provide ideal conditions for launching these engineless aircraft. The thermals created by the ranging hills and dales give the light aircraft a tremendous uplift on rising currents of air, while the views from aloft are staggering in their range and beauty, and the peace they signify.

Since the war, gliding in these elegant sailplanes has become more and more popular and the thriving club now has its own landing strip, runway and control tower, along with administrative and social buildings. There is also a caravan site for its members. By the time I arrived at Aidensfield, the prestige of this club had become such that it hosted events which were of considerable importance in the gliding world — these included both local and national championships, as well as club gliding events and social functions.

During the long, lazy summer which marked the Patringtons' second anniversary in Coltsfoot Cottage, the club hosted the British Long Distance Sailplane Championships.

This attracted a host of enthusiasts to the area who were accommodated at local hotels, inns, boarding-houses and cottages. They swamped the nearby caravan sites and their presence brought wealth to the area. These people had money and cheerfully spent it.

Many of them were from the world of business and commerce and I wondered if James Patrington had joined the Club. As I patrolled my beat during the two weeks of the Championships, I could imagine him soaring aloft in a glider as he enjoyed the solitude and silence of the skies above the North York Moors. Perhaps he was involved, perhaps he wasn't. I did not know.

But, like all previous sailplane championships, there were problems. The more regular of these problems involved a glider coming to earth in an unexpected place. With so many competitors and so many engineless aircraft in the sky, I suppose it is inevitable that some of them fail to remain aloft or cannot make the return journey back to base. The result was that over the two weeks of this event, some six or seven gliders crash-landed around the Club premises. Fortunately, none of these resulted in serious injury to the pilot or anyone else.

I witnessed one of these crash landings. I was patrolling my patch one Saturday afternoon and had parked my Francis Barnett in Crampton. I was performing a short foot patrol around that village and had just emerged from the village shop when my attention was drawn to a whistling sound overhead. And there, floating dangerously low over the village, was a gleaming white glider. It didn't need an expert to realise that it had lost its necessary height, and that it was coming rapidly to earth. To be honest, it was the sort of thing the local people had come to expect and Ryedale does possess many suitable places upon which to safely land.

With the wind hissing about its framework, it came frighteningly low over the chimneys and pantile roofs and it was banking as it circled in a desperate search for a safe landing site. Beyond the village there were flat fields and indeed, there is a disused wartime airfield — I felt sure the pilot was urging his downward floating craft towards that.

As I hurried between the cottages to watch the pilot's frantic efforts to both save the village from danger and to safely bring down his aircraft, I lost sight of the glider. It disappeared behind a row of cottages as I realised it could never regain the air. It was far too low; it had lost all its altitude.

I hurried to my motorcycle, activated the radio and called my Control Room.

"Delta Alpha Two-Nine," I radioed. "Location Crampton. It appears that a glider has crash-landed in the vicinity of Crampton — am investigating. Over."

"Received Two-Nine. Please provide sit-rep as soon as possible. Control out."

With several villagers watching with interest, I motor-cycled out of Crampton towards Brantsford, for that road led into a bewildering array of narrow lanes and tiny hamlets. The glider was last seen heading in that direction; I was sure it had come down somewhere in that maze of lanes and fields, or even on the disused airfield. It could not have flown far and there was no sign of it in the air.

As I drove along the lane which ran through the old disused airfield, there was no sign of the glider, so I turned left and chugged along, sometimes standing on the footrests so that I could peer over the hedges into the large fields on either side. I was now heading for Seavham.

I drove through the hamlet and remained alert for any signs or news that the glider had landed nearby. But there was no one in the street and the Post Office was closed. At least ten minutes had elapsed since my sighting, so I continued through the village and turned left at the end, passing the oval pond which was overlooked by two pretty thatched cottages.

This lane took me on a circular route back to Crampton and I felt that the aircraft couldn't have travelled much further. It hadn't.

As I crested a gentle rise in the lane, I could see its tail sticking into the air like that of a diving whale and I could distinguish one crooked wing behind a copse of sycamore trees. I accelerated now, anxious to save life if that proved necessary, and within a minute was drawing up at the scene of the crash.

I was horrified.

The glider had come down squarely on the top of Coltsfoot Cottage. The nose had penetrated the new-ly-thatched roof and had thrust piles of straw on to the earth around the house.

Both the nose and fuselage were hidden deep inside the walls, while one wing had cracked off completely and was lying in the garden. The other was sticking out of the cot-tage, its fuselage-end deep inside the walls and the slender tip rising awkwardly to the sky like a huge broken feather. And the tail stuck up too, like a sentinel.

For one fleeting moment, I thought it looked like a giant white seagull sitting on a nest, but this was serious.

I parked my motorcycle on the road outside and ran into the grounds. My first contact was with a woman.

She was comforting James Patrington as he sat on the lawn. She saw me approaching.

"Thank God," she said.

"Anyone badly hurt?" was my first question.

"This gentleman's wife," she said. "We were driving past at the time . . . we saw it all . . . my husband's rushed her in his car to the hospital. Brantsford Cottage Hospital . . . she had a knock on the head . . ."

"And the pilot?"

"Him as well, he was bleeding from his face and leg . . . my husband's taken him as well, this gentleman isn't badly hurt. Just shocked, I think. No one's badly hurt."

The first aid training I'd received told me that shock alone could be a severe medical problem, so I radioed Control Room and provided a brief outline of the incident, then asked for an ambulance to take James to hospital as well, for a check-up. The good news was that no one was seriously hurt.

From this point, there would be all kinds of official bodies to inform; all that action would be undertaken by the Force Control Room who would operate from a prearranged set of instructions for dealing with crashed aircraft.

My priority now was to ensure that James received immediate medical attention, and that there was no immediate danger from the aircraft or the house. Happily, there was no aircraft fuel to worry about and there were no fires burning in the house. That reduced the fire risk enormously but it couldn't be ruled out. I decided to keep everyone away from the house and to preserve the scene against the sightseers who would inevitably arrive.

As I marshalled my thoughts I made sure that all the relevant services were notified and that attention was given to the people and the premises. But I could have wept at the sight of the cottage. Perhaps, because it was a thatched roof, it could be repaired fairly easily and likewise because it was a soft landing, there had been no serious injury. It looked a real mess.

Later from home, I rang Brantsford Cottage Hospital to learn that James had suffered severe shock and had been detained. The pilot, a man called Alastair Campbell from Edinburgh, had a broken leg and severe bruising. He had also been detained. I then asked about Mrs Patrington, but the hospital had no record of her. When I added that she was a victim of the glider crash, I was told she had been removed to Scarborough General Hospital for treatment.

As I looked up the telephone number of Scarborough Hospital, my own telephone rang. When I picked up the receiver, a woman's voice asked, "Hello, is that PC Rhea?"

"Speaking," I acknowledged. "Who's that?"

"Lucy Patrington," she responded. "I've just heard the news on the radio, is it true? That a glider's crashed into our cottage?"

I must admit that I was thrown completely off my stride by this call and for a moment, I did not reply. Was she really ringing me to ask this, or was she in hospital, dazed perhaps?

I wondered if the shock of the event had caused her to lose all memories of the crash. Maybe she'd been unsettled by the trauma of the event?

"Hello," she said anew.

"Oh sorry, Mrs Patrington," I apologised, "I was completing something . . . er . . . yes, I'm afraid it is true . . . James is in the Cottage Hospital at Brantsford now, but he's not hurt. Just a check visit. I was about to call and ask after you," I rabbited on. "Now, are you fit to be released . . . I mean, should you be out of bed . . . ?"

"Released, Mr Rhea?" she cried. "What on earth are you talking about? I'm in my shop in London, and James has gone to Scotland for a weekend seminar . . ."

Then her voice trailed away and I knew I had let some sort of cat out of some sort of bag.

"James has not gone to Scotland, has he?" She put to me in no uncertain terms.

"All I know," I told her, "is that he was at the house when the glider came down. Maybe he stopped off *en route* to Scotland? I can confirm that a glider has landed on your roof, and no one is seriously hurt, although there is a good deal of damage . . ."

"The news said a woman had been taken to hospital, Mr Rhea," she pressed me.

"She had gone before I arrived . . . I don't know who she was. I am, at this moment, trying to find out who she is and the extent of her injuries. Perhaps it was someone from the village, visiting the cottage . . ." Rather irrationally and without any real reason, I found myself defending James Patrington.

"Perhaps it was that bitch of a secretary of his," she snapped. "It serves them right!" and she slammed down the telephone.

So because something fell out of the sky, James Patrington's little secret had been revealed to the whole world and a few weeks later, the now deserted cottage, still in its damaged condition, was once again put on the market. I never saw James and Lucy again.

I often wonder if he had his cottage insured.

I was more directly involved in another story of love which came about because of a broken romance. This one was almost as unlikely as the Patrington saga.

At three o'clock one morning, my telephone rang. It was downstairs in the office attached to my house, and its continuous shrilling gradually penetrated my sleep. As I staggered downstairs, I rubbed my eyes and tried to shake myself into clarity of action before I lifted the noisy instrument. It was a call from a kiosk.

"PC Rhea, Aidensfield," I announced, shivering as my bare feet grew cold upon the bare composition floor.

At the other end of the line, coins were inserted and the pipping ceased, then all I could hear was sobbing. I waited for a brief moment, hoping that the person would say something, but the sobbing continued.

"Hello?" I called into the phone. "Hello, this is the police."

It continued and I realised Mary had joined me; she stood at my side, wrapping her dressing-gown tightly around her slim body. She'd had the sense to put on her slippers.

"What is it?" she asked. With late calls of this nature, it was natural to think it was a personal family crisis of some kind.

"Somebody sobbing. Listen," and I passed the handset to her. She listened and passed it back.

"Hello," I tried again and increased the volume of my voice this time, "Hello, this is PC Rhea speaking."

"I want to come and see you," said a faint voice, a female voice, through the sobbing.

"Who is it?" I asked, holding the handset so that Mary could hear both sides of the conversation.

"I must come," continued the voice. "Now, or I'll jump under the train . . ."

"What train? Look, who are you? I want to help you." I had detected a note of real desperation in that voice and did not think it was a joke of any kind. "Where are you?" I added.

"Newcastle Railway Station," she sobbed, "and if you don't say yes, I'm going to jump off the platform . . ."

Mary was hissing in my ear.

"For heaven's sake say yes," she snapped. "Don't string her along, don't make it appear you're not going to help . . ."

"But . . ." I began as my suspicious police mind began thinking all manner of thoughts.

"Do it," said Mary.

"Look," I said to the caller, "I'll welcome you, we'll welcome you, my wife and I. You can come and see me. But how . . ."

"I can get the next train to York." Even now, the sobbing sounded less dramatic.

"Yes, all right," I said, "I'll meet you there, at York Station."

"Thank you, oh, thank you," breathed the voice, sniffing as the sobs subsided. "Oh thank you . . ."

The pips sounded and the call was abruptly ended.

I stared at my handset and asked Mary, "Well, what do you make of that?"

She shrugged her shoulders. "One of your ex-girlfriends getting worked up about something? A blast from the past? Or have you been misbehaving when you've been away on your various courses? Maybe you've broken someone's little heart?" There was a trusting twinkle in Mary's eye, but I knew that this call could have been misconstrued in all kinds of ways.

"I don't know who she is or what she wants!" I began a weak protest . . .

"Then you'll have to go to York and find out. Bring her here," said Mary. "She sounds as if she needs help and friendship, whoever she is and whatever she's done."

There are times when one is thankful for a marvellous, understanding wife who possesses oceans of common sense, and this was such a time. Policemen especially require wives who have all the qualities of angels coupled with a high measure of earthly common sense. So, in response to Mary's advice I nodded in agreement and said, "OK, I'll have a cup of tea and get dressed. I'll drive to York to meet our mystery lady."

It was then that I realised it was a Sunday and it should have been my day off. However, I checked the arrival times of trains from Newcastle and as I drove into York in my own car, I wondered whether this was classed as police duty. Was this a private matter or could I claim that I had used my car for emergency duty purposes?

If such thoughts seemed petty, this is not so because if I had an accident on this trip, it would be vital to my future security as to whether or not it was a 'duty' commitment. But there was nothing I could do about the technicalities of the situation at this stage; I would worry about those kind of things after I had met my damsel in distress.

And so it was, that shortly after 4.30 a.m. that chill but sunny Sunday morning, I was standing on York Station awaiting the Newcastle train. I must admit that I wondered whether I was a fool or not, or whether this was some curious prank, but on reflection I knew I had no alternative but to turn out. I had to discover for myself the reality of the situation.

The train was about ten minutes late. A few minutes after its arrival, as I stood at the ticket-collector's barrier, I noticed a young woman heading my way. I did not recognise her. In her late teens or early twenties, she was pretty without being beautiful, and had mousy hair which straggled down to her shoulders. She was dressed in a rather crumpled, short tartan skirt, a dark green velvet top and white blouse. She wore no stockings or tights and was waif-like in many ways. As she drew closer, I could see that her pale face bore a hint of freckles, but other than some pale lipstick she wore no make-up. She had no luggage or topcoat but did carry a black handbag.

After passing through the barrier, she managed an embarrassed smile as she came nervously towards me. She was like a naughty child who was anticipating a telling-off by an angry parent.

"Hello." Clearly she knew who I was. She stood before me like a lost kitten.

"Hello," I returned, racking my brains in an attempt to recall her name or where we'd met. In those few brief moments, I failed. I had no idea who she was.

"I'm sorry . . . for all this . . ." she began in an accent which I did not recognise as either Yorkshire or Tyneside. "I was silly . . . I'll go back. I'm all right now." She turned to walk away from me.

"No," I said, still baffled. "Don't go. You need help, don't you? Look, my car's outside and my wife has got a cup of tea ready. The buffet's closed, I'm afraid, so we can't talk here."

"No," she said, "I'm all right now, honest. I can go. I'll go back to Newcastle on the next train . . . I was silly . . . I'm confused . . . I'm a nuisance to you."

"No," I said, "my wife wants to meet you and I want to know what all this is about. So, come along. No arguing! I'm here because I want to help you."

She hesitated momentarily, then followed me to my waiting car. Without a word, she climbed into the passenger-seat and settled down as I drove through York's deserted streets.

"Well," I said as we cleared the town, "so what's all this about? How about a name to start with?"

"Tessa," she said. "Teresa, really, but everybody calls me Tessa. Tessa Underwood."

"I'm still baffled," I admitted. "I don't recall that name. Tell me about the phone call, Tessa. You wanted help, so why did you ring me? I don't know you."

"It all sounds so silly now, Mr Rhea," she used my name quite normally. "It really does. After the train ride, I came to my senses. It was so silly . . . I feel a right fool, I do, bothering you like this, when you don't know me."

"It wasn't silly at three o'clock this morning, Tessa. It was very serious then, and it could be serious again so let's hear about it."

And so, during the half-hour trip from York to Aidensfield, I managed to drag the story from her. Brought up in Staffordshire, her parents had been killed in a road accident about four years ago, when she was seventeen. For a time, she'd lived with an aunt, but had fallen out with her. So eighteen months ago, she had moved to Newcastle-upon-Tyne where she now worked as a shorthand typist in a factory on a new industrial estate.

She lived alone in a little flat which she rented and, apart from Mark, her boyfriend, and some of the girls at work, she knew no one. Some of the girls at work had made fun of her because of her curious accent, but three days ago, her boyfriend had left her.

At this stage, the tears started again; I was tempted to halt the car and comfort her but felt it wiser to continue. I exhorted her to continue. Through her sobs, she said Mark left her for a married woman he'd met in a night club, a real old scrubber according to Tessa. All attempts at reconciliation had failed; Tessa, with no parents to turn to and no relations other than the awkward aunt, felt she could not confide in anyone. She was alone in the world; She'd felt unloved and unwanted.

In her own way, she provided me with a graphic account of how her misery and loneliness had turned into a suicidal determination. Burdened with her worries in the early hours of this very morning, she had gone down to Newcastle Central railway station with a determination to throw herself under one of the speeding expresses. Even now, as she re-told her story among floods of tears, she wondered how she could have contemplated such a thing.

"I wasn't thinking straight," she said. "It was horrid. I was . . . oh . . . so silly, so miserable and sad, lonely . . . it was Saturday night, you see, and everyone goes out with friends and I had none, only Mark, and he'd left me . . . I had no one, Mr Rhea. No one. If you hadn't said you'd see me . . ."

"But I did. I said you could come to see me and here you are. If that action has stopped you from doing something

55

silly, then I'm delighted. Now, do you think you've got rid of those awful thoughts?"

She nodded and wiped her eyes. "I'll be all right now."

"But," this was the point that still puzzled me, "why ring me? Of all the people who would have helped — the local police, for example, the Salvation Army, the Church! And you rang me!"

She produced a thin smile and looked embarrassed. "It was so good of you, I mean, you could have said no and . . ."

"And you might have jumped in front of a train?"

"You didn't ignore me, Mr Rhea . . . I'm . . . well . . ."

"I know. But, Tessa, I don't know you. I still can't understand why you rang me?"

She hesitated. We were now drawing close to Aidensfield and in the growing light of dawn, I could distinguish my police house on its lofty site which overlooked the ranging and beautiful countryside. By now, it was after five o'clock and the lights of some houses were showing as smoke rose from our chimney. Mary had prepared a welcome for this girl.

"Can you remember a car breaking down outside your house, about a year ago?" Tessa asked, smiling at the memory.

Vaguely, I did recall the incident.

"Me and . . . that boy . . . well, we'd had a day out on the moors in his car, and when we came along the road somewhere in this area, we found a small suitcase lying in the road. So we picked it up and thought we'd better report it to the police. Well, yours was the first police station we saw. So we stopped and Mark, that's him, made me bring it in."

I was now recalling the incident with more clarity.

"He didn't want to bring it in, so I did. I handed it to you and you made a note of it in case the loser came asking."

"She did, I remember," I said. "She was most grateful — it had fallen off a roof-rack. So that was you, was it? You look so different!"

"I've changed — I've lost my puppy fat for one thing, and I've had my hair cut."

"So you remembered me from that little incident?"

"Well, you remember Mark's car? When I went back to the car after bringing in the suitcase it wouldn't start. Mark tried and tried, so you ran him down to a garage in the village and got a set of plugs or something for the engine."

"Points," I corrected her. "A set of points. Yes, and we put them in, me and your friend. I remember it now."

"Well," she was still trying to reach the end of her story, "I remembered how helpful you were . . ."

"It was nothing," I said.

"But you see, I wasn't used to policemen helping me, Mark neither. But, well, I kept the receipt you gave me for that suitcase. It was in my handbag, it has been there ever since. You know what women are for carrying stuff around and well, last night when I was so unhappy and depressed, I was rifling through my bag, getting rid of his letters and things at the station. I was putting things in the rubbish bin, you know, getting rid of everything, then I found that receipt. It had your number on as well. So I rang — and here I am."

"I'm pleased you rang if it meant so much," I was sincere. "Well, we're almost home."

"I'll go straight back," she said. "I shouldn't have come. I've been a silly, stupid nuisance and I've thought things out on that train, sensibly I think. I had time . . ."

"At least come in and have some breakfast," I offered. "And you are welcome to stay until you get yourself completely sorted out."

And so she did. At Mary's invitation, she stayed three days and Mary was marvellous with her. Tessa was lovely with our children too, and that girl and our family are still good friends. She still calls, albeit now with a new husband and two lovely children of her own.

But her presence in our house did cause a flutter of interest and some speculation in the village. Mary and I decided we must not tell anyone of her real reason for being with us, and so we were faced with questions like, "Is that the wife's sister then?" or "Been arrested, has she?" or "Is she a policewoman in disguise, watching summat in Aidensfield?"

In all cases, we simply said she was a friend who was staying for a day or two.

But I often wonder whether that event was part of my police duty or not. I think not, for I never mentioned it to any of my superiors.

CHAPTER 4

Little deeds of kindness, little words of love
Help to make the earth happy, like the heaven above.
JULIA CARNEY, 1823—1908

There was a great excitement in Ashfordly one Friday morning in June. It arose because BBC radio had decided to broadcast its 'Good Morning' programme from a mobile studio in the market-place. It was to be a live broadcast from the North Region and would be on the air from 7 a.m. until 9 a.m. At that time, the 'Good Morning' series visited a different town or village each week and the series had a dedicated following.

It was natural that the people of Ashfordly were excited and delighted that their charming market town had been selected and in due course, a list of candidates for interview was drawn up. Personalities from all walks of life were procured and the interviews would be interspersed with music and reports about a selection of the interesting places in the locality.

Late on the Thursday afternoon beforehand, the BBC's entourage arrived and the galaxy of technicians and production staff established themselves and their vehicles at the prearranged place. The little town awaited the honour of tomorrow's spell of publicity, while the participants grew more nervous as their hour of glory approached. The police, as always, had their role to play.

In addition to keeping a protective eye on the vehicles and their loads of expensive equipment during the preceding night, they had to maintain a discreet presence on the day itself. We had to be there just in case someone tried to gatecrash the proceedings or otherwise make a nuisance of themselves.

As an outdoor audience was anticipated in the vicinity of the mobile studio, there would be a degree of crowd control and some car-parking to supervise. Duties of this kind were undertaken in conjunction with every crowd-pulling event and the BBC's 'Good Morning from Ashfordly' was no exception. As our duty rota had been compiled some weeks in advance, I was delighted to find that I was to perform an early morning patrol that Friday. My duties were from 6 a.m. until 9 a.m. and I was therefore allocated a foot patrol in the town centre so that a uniformed police presence would be evident.

I looked forward to the work.

I left home at six o'clock on my Francis Barnett, arrived at Ashfordly Police Station at 6.15 a.m. and left my motorcycle there. I also left my motorcycling weather-proof clothes and donned my uniform cap as I set about my patrol. Even at that early stage of the morning, a small crowd of onlookers had gathered but they stood at a respectful distance and appeared to be causing no bother. The technicians were hard at work setting up and checking their sophisticated equipment while the producer of the programme had gathered the programme participants in a separate caravan for a final briefing.

I did not intrude. I could see that things were moving apace so I kept in the background, watchful but discreet. The minutes ticked away and then, as seven o'clock approached, much of the crowd melted away.

I realised they would be going home to hear the broadcast and I wondered if Sergeant Blaketon would be listening.

He had not yet made an appearance and I did wonder if he was just a wee bit upset because he was not one of the selected personalities . . . But I reckoned he would be tuned in as he enjoyed his breakfast.

I knew that I could listen to parts of the broadcast in a friendly bakery just behind the market-place. Confident that my presence was not required, I sidled away and entered the bakery by a side door. I was assailed by the marvellous whiff of new bread as the manager noticed my entry. He pointed to the kettle and then to a radio perched on a shelf.

I got the message. They were listening as they worked, and I was invited to join them and to make myself a cup of tea; they were already drinking theirs. I asked if anyone required a refill, but they were content and made hand signals to inform me of the fact, so I made myself a cup and stood in silence beneath the radio. At seven, the broadcast started with the announcer sounding bright and breezy as he introduced the programme and gave a brief résumé of Ashfordly's topography and the delights in store.

Then he said, "And here I am, in the middle of the market-place awaiting my guests. And in my rush to get everything ready this morning, I forgot to bring some sugar for my tea! We've no sugar in the studio, folks, but perhaps someone will fetch a spoonful along . . ."

No one in the bakery made a move, and so I decided to help out. After all, I reasoned, everyone else was glued to their radios at home, and would hate to move away in case they missed something. If everyone took this attitude, no one would provide the sugar! And so I thanked the bakery staff for the tea and left. The shops which stocked sugar would not yet be open, so I hurried to the police station, located the tin of sugar we used in our own tea-swindle, and poured some into a milk bottle.

Rather than carry it through the streets in my uniform I donned my crash helmet, popped the bottle of sugar into the pannier of my motorcycle and scooted the few yards back to the market-place. Lifting the machine on to its stand, I removed the bottle of sugar and walked across to the BBC's collection of vehicles. At the door of the studio, I found an assistant, handed over the sugar with my compliments and left.

I returned to my bike, placed the crash helmet upon the saddle and resumed a normal patrol. And that, I thought, was that. It was my good deed for the day. Twenty minutes later, I was in the local newsagent's shop, a courtesy visit during my patrol, and I heard the broadcast issuing from their radio.

Miss Phyllis Oakworth, a leading light in Ashfordly WI for fifty years, had just been interviewed, and the announcer was once again in full flow.

And to my horror, I heard him say, "I am delighted that my plea for some sugar has been answered. I've now got enough for myself and my guests. For this, my thanks go to the local constabulary in Ashfordly who rushed a supply to our studio by police motorcycle. Now there's an example of co-operation between the police and the public — if you need help, just ask an Ashfordly policeman. Well done, Officer, whoever you were, you've saved the day. I think your policemen are wonderful, Ashfordly. And now to our next guest . . ."

"You?" asked Ken, the newsagent.

I nodded and grimaced at the unwarranted publicity, but he just laughed. "Nice one," he said and continued his work among the morning papers.

I left the shop and wondered who, among the dozens of my senior officers, had heard that; furthermore, I wondered what their reaction would be. Could my action be construed as too frivolous for a police officer? But as the morning passed and the local folks listened to their own town, its people and its attractions being so professionally scrutinised, my worries began to evaporate.

Then, at quarter to nine, I noticed the tall, smart but severe figure of Sergeant Blaketon as he moved towards me across the market square. Rigidly upright and with military bearing, he came towards me, an impressive man in his immaculate uniform. He was prominent among the crowd which had grown larger due to the arrival of some workers who were due to start their day's toil at nine o'clock.

They had paused for a moment before disappearing into their offices and places of work, and the broadcast was drawing to a close in those final minutes.

"All correct, Rhea?" he asked. I noticed the more-serious-than-usual expression on his face as he arrived at my side.

"All correct, Sergeant," I responded in the traditional manner.

"No problems? Trouble from the crowd? Parking?"

"No, Sergeant."

"No crimes, no pickpockets in the crowd, no thieves at work as everyone's attention was diverted by this affair?"

"No, Sergeant," I said, hoping that no one had taken the opportunity to steal a bike or to take someone's wallet. That sort of thing just did not happen in Ashfordly, I felt, and so I was confident in my bland assessment of the situation.

"No overnight break-ins? Car thefts? Broken windows not discovered?"

"No, Sergeant," and my answer must, by this time, have sounded quizzical. He was going on a bit, I felt, certainly more than usual. In normal circumstances, my "All Correct" speech would have been sufficient, but he was probing now. I realised he was leading up to something; judging by the expression on his face, it was something serious. I began to wonder if a crime *had* been reported or if some incident had occurred. If so, I was not aware of it and that could infer that I had neglected my duty.

Somewhat worried by his attitude, we made a brief perambulation of the market square and I noticed that the crowd was now dwindling as the people finally went to their places of work.

"If you have been so vigilant, Rhea, and have had such a positive command of the situation, how is it that you have found the time to be entertained by a radio programme?"

"Sergeant?"

He came to a halt in a quiet recess near the town hall and we stood together as he mustered his speech. "The sugar, Rhea. There am I, sitting at my breakfast-table, when I learn that one of my constables has heard a plea for sugar from this lot here, these broadcasting people. That alone indicates that the constable in question must have been neglecting his duty, that he was failing to work his beat in accordance with instructions . . ."

"I . . ." I couldn't believe what I was hearing.

"And furthermore," his voice rose to stifle any comment I might make, "there is the question of the misuse of police vehicles, that is, the use of an official motorcycle and fuel, to say nothing of police time, to convey the sugar from the police office to these broadcasting people, and there is also the question of the ownership of the sugar, eh Rhea? Was it yours to give away? Was it your personal property? Or was it sugar which belonged to the Police Authority? Was it sugar from a fund of some kind?"

"But, Sergeant — "

"And on top of all that, Rhea, how do you think the public will react to this? Will those listeners, those thousands or even millions of them out there, think that Ashfordly Police have nothing better to do than to act as delivery men for the BBC? We will be the laughing-stock of police forces, Rhea, we will be the butt of jokes from our city counterparts who are coping with murders and mayhem. They will now believe that we occupy our duty time by running cupfuls of official sugar from police stations to broadcasting people who then announce it to the world . . ."

Sergeant Oscar Blaketon was on top form. All his prejudices and formal police attitudes were emerging as he stood there in the recess near the town hall, giving vent to his concern.

"But, Sergeant . . ."

"And Rhea, let us now suppose that the Superintendent or even the Chief Constable himself was listening to that programme! What are they to think about it all, Rhea? How am I to justify your actions; your highly unofficial and thoughtless actions; your neglect of duty in this very public manner; your misuse of police property . . ."

"Sergeant, I thought — "

"I don't care what you thought, Rhea. What I do care about is what you did. And what you did could amount to a breach of the Discipline Code with the severest of repercussions for you and for the Force . . ."

I must admit I had not for one moment thought of that aspect. Anyone else, in any sort of job or profession, would have done the same, so why should the police be any different? But, according to Blaketon's interpretation of the Police (Discipline) Regulations, it did seem that I had fallen foul of those rules, and I knew him well enough to realise that he would have checked the provisions of that code before coming to speak to me. He was not the man to leave such detail to chance.

As he continued his diatribe, I visualised the punishments that could be imposed for such breaches of the Discipline Regulations. There was dismissal from the Force, with an alternative of a requirement to resign; there was reduction in rank (which didn't apply to me because, as a constable, I was at the bottom of the scale); a reduction in pay; a fine; a reprimand or a caution.

I began to feel pale and sick and started to worry about my future, both in the immediate and long term. I knew the Discipline Code was strict and that some supervisory officers reinforced it to the letter . . .

"So, Rhea," said Blaketon as he concluded his lecture, "you will submit a report about his incident. In triplicate. And it will be on my desk not later than twelve noon today."

"Yes, Sergeant," I said, with evident meekness.

Having delivered his lecture, he strode away, grim-faced, awesome yet somehow majestic in his unassailable attitude. With my mind ranging across the problem I had now created for myself, I watched the BBC technicians begin to dismantle their equipment and decided I was no longer required. I went across to my motorcycle and mounted it.

A voice called to me from the assembled BBC personnel. "Thanks for the sugar, Officer!"

"Cheers!" I responded with a wave of my hand and knew I dare not tell them of Blaketon's reaction or of my impending ordeal. Communication with journalists about internal police matters was another disciplinary offence, so I left it at that. Dejected and worried, I started the Francis Barnett and motored slowly back to Aidensfield.

Over breakfast, I told Mary all about it and she thought it was a ridiculous attitude, but at ten o'clock I settled in my office to type the report. I knew it must be totally factual and that I should not try to make excuses; I therefore decided on a plain, simple and honest account of my sugar mission. I would set it out in chronological order.

At twenty minutes past ten, my telephone rang.

"PC Rhea, Aidensfield," I announced.

"Just a moment," said a woman's voice at the other end of the line, "I have the Chief Constable for you."

I nearly fell off my chair. The Chief! I saw myself being summoned immediately to Police Headquarters to account for my actions. I saw myself writing out my resignation and looking for another job. My heart thumped as I waited for the great man to speak.

I tried to marshal my thoughts in an attempt to justify my actions. I clung to the telephone, nervous and worried, as his secretary connected me.

"Chief Constable," I heard his crisp response.

"PC Rhea, Aidensfield, sir," I answered.

"Ah, Rhea. I have been in touch with your Divisional Headquarters and they tell me that you were the constable on duty at Ashfordly this morning."

"Yes, sir," I admitted, quaking.

"And am I right in thinking that you were responsible for supplying some sugar to the BBC during that morning broadcast?"

I swallowed. So he had been listening, just as old Blaketon had feared.

"Yes, sir," my voice must have sounded faint and weak as I croaked my reply.

"Bloody good show!" he said. "That was an excellent piece of public relations, Rhea. It gave the police a sympathetic and human image, and I was delighted it was my force which had done it. Excellent, well done. I just wanted you to know that I was delighted, and so was the Government Inspector. He heard the broadcast too and was delighted. He has just called me."

And so, in one single moment, all my worries and tensions evaporated.

"It's good of you to ring, sir . . ." I managed to splutter.

"Not at all. It's the least I could do. Keep up the good work, Rhea," and he ended our conversation.

I sat in my chair as a feeling of release swept over me. Now, I had the perfect ending for my report to Sergeant Blaketon.

To conclude it, I added this sentence, "At 10.20 a.m. today, I received a telephone call from the Chief Constable who had heard the broadcast in question. He congratulated me on my actions and stressed the public relations value of the publicity. The HMI also expressed his pleasure in similar terms and had conveyed his appreciation to the Chief Constable with a request that it be transmitted to me."

At half past eleven, I signed my report and drove into Ashfordly with it. Sergeant Blaketon was on the telephone as I walked into the office, so I placed my report on his desk and walked out.

Never again did he refer to the matter.

On another occasion, it was the police who needed assistance and I found myself involved in that episode too. The ingredients were an ancient ruined abbey, a religious service, some severe car-parking problems and a stubborn Yorkshire farmer.

In the spring of the year, Ashfordly Police Station received a visit from Father Geoffrey Summerson, the Roman Catholic parish priest. Sergeant Bairstow was on duty at the time and warmly received his visitor.

Father Summerson was a small man who had passed his sixtieth birthday; he had been at Ashfordly for many years and ran a happy, busy little parish. He was constantly involved in events and happenings in the town and his diminutive, but powerful personality made him popular with all faiths and even with those who professed no known religion.

His frail figure, with a somewhat gaunt and hungry appearance, belied a bundle of energy which he used for the good of both the town and his parishioners. At first sight, he looked humourless and severe, with a sallow skin drawn tight over thin, high cheekbones. Small, pale eyes glinted from behind rimless spectacles and his hands were never still. He was fond of gesticulations; constantly emphasising his words with sweeping gestures or meaningful movements of his thin arms and surprisingly long and slender hands. They were the hands of an artist or musician but I do not know whether he possessed either of those talents.

That day, however, he arrived at the police station on foot, clad in his dark grey suit and dog collar. I was on the telephone at the time, receiving a long, involved message about warble fly. I saw the priest being invited into the sergeant's office and guessed it indicated a matter of some importance.

I concluded my call and at a wink from the sergeant, put on the kettle for some coffee.

"Well, Father," Sergeant Bairstow was always happy and cheerful, "what can we do for you this bright, spring morning?"

"Good of you to see me, Sergeant," began the priest. "It's about Waindale Abbey. It is within your province, isn't it?"

"Yes," said Bairstow. "It's on our patch."

Waindale Abbey is one of several beautiful ruins dotted around the area. Wrecked by the Commissioners of Henry VIII during the Reformation, it sits beside the gentle River Wain where its impressive location and magnificent broken outline give testimony to its dramatic past. Today, it is a popular tourist attraction where its mellow stone and lofty columns give no hint of the role it once played in the economic life of the locality.

"This year marks the thirteenth centenary of the foundation of the Abbey," began the priest. "It is one of the oldest ruins in the land and dates to the earliest times of Christendom in this country. So," he went on, "we — that is the hierarchy of the Catholic Church, with the blessing of members of the Anglican faith I might add — have decided to mark the occasion. We are going to hold a Concelebrated Mass with the bishop and priests of this diocese. It will take place in the ruins and the proposed date is 24 August, that's the Feast of St Bartholomew, patron saint of the Abbey."

"So that will mean a considerable influx of people and vehicles, Father?"

"Yes, I estimate there'll be well into tens of thousands. Bus loads, cars, foot and cycle pilgrims, priests, nuns and laity — they'll come from all the northern parishes and even further afield. That is why I am here, to give you due notice, so that you can make your own plans."

I took them a cup of coffee each and settled down in the front office to enjoy one too. They continued their chat and I could hear every word. It was not a confidential meeting.

"We appreciate adequate warning, Father, then we can arrange our duties to cope. Will you want a police presence inside the Abbey grounds, do you think, or merely on the outside to cope with the traffic and crowds?"

"Certainly on the outside, Sergeant. As for the interior, well, I imagine our pilgrims will behave, although a discreet police presence is never amiss."

"I'll mark the date in our duty diary," said Sergeant Bairstow. "You'll not have the time of the service yet?"

"No, those matters are to be finalized, but it will be during the afternoon, probably beginning at 2.30 p.m. or 3.00 p.m. But some people will arrive much earlier; some will bring picnics, I know, and they will give the day a holiday atmosphere, a form of celebration."

"Good, well, Father, thank you for this advance notice. You'll keep in touch please, about the timing and other details?"

"Of course, and don't hesitate to contact me if there's anything more you need to know."

Father Summerson left and Sergeant Bairstow came into the front office. "You heard all that, Nick?" he asked.

I nodded. "It looks like being a busy day."

"You're telling me! There'll be lost children to consider; wandering old ladies; lost and found property; toilet facilities to provide; car and coach parking . . . There'll be other traffic in the valley, trying to squeeze past the pilgrims on those narrow lanes, and the local residents will play hell about it all. We'll have to ensure access for any emergency vehicles and there'll be litter; first aid facilities to think about; possible crimes like pickpockets or other thefts . . ."

"It'll keep us busy for weeks!" I laughed.

"And for that remark, young Rhea, consider yourself involved right from the start! Right now, in fact. Come along, we'll go and inspect the scene, shall we?"

In the Sergeant's official car, we drove the four miles or so across the hills and into the valley of Waindale. The lanes were peaceful, with the hedges just bursting into the fresh green leaf, while the fields and woodlands were changing into their spring colours. Flowers like wild daffodils and celandines adorned the verges and birds sang in marvellous harmony as we dropped down the steep incline into the lovely valley. To give the monks due praise, they certainly knew how to select an ideal site.

The tiny village with its cluster of yellow stone cottages, some thatched and others with red pantile roofs, reclined beneath the shadow of the hillside, while the magnificent Abbey occupied a huge, flat site deep in the valley.

"You know, Nick," breathed Sergeant Bairstow, "this view never ceases to thrill me. It really is incredible, those woods, the fields, the river down there — see? And the Abbey, silent and just a little mysterious . . . I've seen it with a mist around it at dawn; I've seen it at night in the light of a full moon, and at sunset too . . ."

I knew what he was trying to say. There was a magic about the place, an indefinable atmosphere rich with the scents of history and drama and it was something I'd experienced on the occasions I'd come here.

We eased our little police car into the car park and emerged to breathe the crisp, fresh air of Waindale.

"And to think we get paid for this!" smiled Sergeant Bairstow. "Come along, let's have a critical look at the interior."

After explaining our purpose to the lady in the little wooden hut at the entrance, we walked around as we tried to envisage how the huge congregation would be accommodated; where the altar should be sited both for safety and for vision. We wondered whether crowd-barriers were needed and which was the best place to site the portable toilets, the first aid centre, the lost children tent and other essentials.

We had to ensure that the village was free to go about its normal business, and we must be equally sure that ambulances could gain access to any possible casualties in the crowd. Thoughts of this kind were part of any exploratory visit and Sergeant Bairstow was sufficiently experienced to be aware of the requirements. We both knew that an Operation Order would be needed to cope with all the problems of the day, and as a plan formed in his mind, he decided it was an ideal opportunity to make use of our band of local, dedicated special constables.

My next contact with Father Summerson came through a telephone call. I was in Ashfordly at the time and accepted the call.

"It's Father Summerson," he said. "I'm ringing about the Abbey celebrations."

"It's PC Rhea, Father. I am familiar with the event so far."

"Good, well I thought you'd better know that we have received some intelligence from our parishes. At this stage, we believe that the congregation will be in excess of 20,000 — it might even rise to 30,000. I thought you had better be aware of these numbers."

I found it difficult to visualise such a crowd in Waindale Abbey, and expressed that point.

"Oh, the Abbey will accommodate them," he said with some assurance. "There is plenty of space. It is the traffic that worries me, Constable. From what I hear, most will be coming by coach but there will be many cars."

I realised that the volume of incoming traffic would be similar to that which arrives at a popular race meeting, but this was no racetrack and there was a distinct lack of parking space. There were none of the facilities necessary for coping with such numbers. In short, we, and the church organisers, were to be faced with a car-parking problem of some magnitude. It could not be left to chance or ignored.

I thanked him for this advance information and wrote the details on a note for the attention of Sergeant Bairstow. He contacted me a couple of days later and said, "Nick, I'll pick you up at half past nine this morning. We'll have another look at Waindale Abbey — it's about the parking problems."

We stood in the centre of the tiny official car park and calculated that it would accommodate no more than twenty cars — and at an average of four persons per car, that was a mere eighty people.

"That'll just about cater for the official party," Bairstow said. "And there's nowhere else. They can't park in these lanes — they'd be blocked in no time. So young Nicholas, what are we to do?"

"We could organise parking elsewhere and bus them in here," I suggested.

"Have you ever tried that? It causes chaos and delays. Besides, don't forget many of these folks will not be in organised parties. They'll drive to the dale in their own transport, and they'll come right here. We have no control over them."

"There is a field about a hundred yards away," I told him. "Just beyond that cottage and small-holding."

"Flat, is it? And dry?"

"I think so. We can inspect it now," I suggested.

We walked along the lane towards an old stone cottage with smoke rising from its chimney. Hens clucked in the yard and there was a goat tethered among the apple trees in a small orchard. An elderly woman was sweeping the doorstep with a large stiff brush and Sergeant Bairstow addressed her.

"Excuse me," he said. "This field? Do you know whose it is?"

"Aye," she said. "Awd Arthur Craggs. Up yonder," and she pointed to a farmhouse almost hidden by trees. It overlooked the valley and the Abbey from its elevated site.

"Thanks."

The field was ideal. There were two wide entrances, one at each end. Each was large enough to permit coaches and cars to turn off the lane as they entered the valley from both directions. It was a large, flat area of grass which had once been two fields, and the surface was solid. We tramped across it, testing the ground with our heels and trying to estimate how many vehicles it would contain.

"Even if it rains," I said "this surface will be sound enough. They won't get bogged down — it's solid enough to take the buses, isn't it?"

"I reckon it is, Nick. It's just what we need. But it won't rain," chuckled Bairstow. "I have it on good authority! Father Summerson says he's praying for a fine day. He assures me it will be fine and that there will be no rain and no weather problems. He's not even thinking of a wet weather programme or an awning for the altar!"

"That's faith for you!" I said. "But God works in mysterious ways!"

"Then let's hope he approves of this field as a car park!"

We decided not to take the car up to Arthur Craggs' farm, but walked up the steep, unmade track and found ourselves in an expansive and rather untidy farmyard. Other than a few bantams pecking for scraps, there was no sign of life, so we went to the house. The door was open so we knocked and shouted, and a woman called, "T'dooer's oppen."

We knew it was an invitation and so we stepped in. A farmer and his wife were sitting at a large, scrubbed kitchen table, each with a mug of tea and a huge slice of cake before them.

"Sit down," she said without waiting for any introductions and went across to the kettle which was boiling on the Aga. Being familiar with the customary hospitality of the local farmers, we settled on chairs at the table, and she produced a mug of hot tea and a massive chunk of fruit cake for each of us. We weren't given the luxury of plates.

"Is it about me stock register?" said the man.

"No," said Sergeant Bairstow. "Are you Arthur Craggs?"

"There's neearbody else of that name lives here," he said, grinning widely and showing a mouthful of stained and rotten teeth. He would be in his late sixties, I reckoned, a ruddy-faced man with a few days growth of beard around his jowls and chin. His eyes were light grey and clear and he wore rough working clothes, corduroy trousers with leather leggings and hob-nailed boots. We had arrived at 'owance time', as they called their mid-morning break and even though this couple did not know us, we were expected to share their food. His wife, a plain and simple woman, now settled at the table but did not speak.

"Well," said Sergeant Bairstow, "this is lovely cake and a welcome cup of tea."

"Thoo'll 'ave cum aboot summat else, though?" Those eyes flashed cheekily, playfully even. He knew we wanted some favour from him.

"Yes. You'll have heard that a service is planned in the Abbey, in August."

"Aye," he said, those sharp eyes watching us.

"Well," said the sergeant, "we are looking for somewhere to park the buses and cars. We understand that the field just this side of the Abbey belongs to you."

"Aye," he said, not volunteering anything.

"Well," said Sergeant Bairstow, "we wondered if you would permit the church authorities to use it as a car and coach-park, just for that one afternoon."

"And dis thoo think they'd let me graze my cattle and sheep in yon Abbey, then? There's some nice grass in there. Or mebbe they might let me use yan o' their choches or chapils as a cattle shed, eh?" and he laughed at his own jokes. "Christians share things, deearn't they?"

It was clear we were dealing with a difficult and stubborn old character, but Sergeant Bairstow plodded on.

"It would be needed all day, I reckon," he said. "On 24th August, it's a few months away yet, but we need to be finalizing our plans . . ."

"Well, Sergeant," he said, sipping from his mug. "Ah might 'ave sheep in yon field by then, or coos, or even some beeasts Ah might be aiming o' buying. There again, Ah might decide to put some poultry 'uts in there . . . thoo sees, Sergeant, Ah 'm a busy farmer and my lands are needed all t' time, for summat or even for summat else. All's allus shifting things about . . . nivver stops . . ."

"It would be required only for that one day . . ."

"Yar day's t'same as onny other in my mind," he said. "It maks neea difference what day it is. Besides, Sergeant, Ah's nut a Catholic, and it's them lot that wants to come, isn't it?"

"I expect there'll be pilgrims of all faiths on the day," Sergeant Bairstow said truthfully.

"Well," said Craggs, "Ah's nut gahin to say they can 'ave yon field. It's a lang while off yit, and Ah just might want to use it mesell."

And he got up from the table.

With that note of finality, we made a move towards the door, and Sergeant Bairstow added, "Thanks for the lowance. But can we ask you to think about it? For the good of the village, really, to keep all the traffic off the roads?"

"Aye," said Arthur Craggs, with those eyes twinkling and almost mocking us. "Thoo can ask me ti think aboot it."

We said nothing to each other until we were clear of his premises, and then Bairstow sighed. "By, Nick, there's some stubborn old mules around these parts. We need a decision from him — a 'yes' decision I might add — before we can go ahead with the planning of this. Do you know him?"

I shook my head. I didn't. I'd never had cause to visit this farm, and so Sergeant Bairstow decided to ask someone else to make an approach to the farmer. Rather craftily, he discovered that Craggs had married in the Waindale Methodist Chapel and therefore asked the local Methodist minister to plead with Craggs. But this failed too. The cunning old farmer refused to commit himself one way or the other.

His indecision created an enormous problem for the organisers and for us. We began to look at several other alternatives for car and coach parking, all grossly inconvenient but vitally necessary.

And then, in late June, Sergeant Bairstow received a very unexpected telephone call.

"It's Craggs," said the voice. "That field. Ah sha'n't be needing it on t'day of yon service. Thoo can 'ave it, Sergeant. Mak sure t' gates is shut when you've finished wiv it," and he put down the telephone.

The relief was tremendous, and the arrangements went ahead with a new impetus. And then the big day dawned. It was fine and warm, a beautiful day as Father Summerson had predicted. During the previous week, the church authorities had fulfilled their role; the signs, toilets, first aid, lost children and lost property — everything had been fixed in readiness and the huge empty field bore enormous signs proclaiming it as the 'Car and Coach-Park'.

Until lunchtime, things went very smoothly. Then, as the time for the commencement of the service approached, the traffic intensified. With an hour to go, the tiny valley and its narrow lanes were congested with slow-moving vehicles, all heading for the car park. Special constables and regular officers were guiding them along and ensuring none parked on the verges or roadside, but the queue grew longer and longer. There was clearly a delay of some kind at the head of the queue.

"Nick," Sergeant Bairstow had come to investigate the problem. "Pop along and see what the hold-up is."

When I arrived at the field, I soon discovered the reason. Farmer Craggs had positioned himself at one entrance, and his wife was at the other; each was equipped with a card-table and a money-box and they had erected crude hand-painted notices which said, 'Parking, Coaches £3; cars 10/-; motor-cycles 5/-; pedal cycles 1 shilling' and they were taking a fortune.

The queues, which extended in both directions from the gates, were the result of motorists and coach drivers pausing while having to pay. I had no idea whether this was part of the deal which had been struck over the use of this field and knew I could not intervene. It was private premises. But the queue was lengthening and the delayed people would inter-rupt the Mass by their late arrival. I suggested to the passen-gers in several cars and coaches that they disembark now, before parking, and so they did. Others copied them, and soon we had a steady stream of pilgrims entering the ruins of this hallowed place as the drivers waited to park.

When I returned to the entrance, I found Sergeant Bairstow talking to Father Summerson.

"Well, Nick?"

I explained the cause of the hold-up, and Father Summerson grimaced. "The crafty old character!" he said. "He demanded a fee from us too and now he's charging the drivers!"

I could see it all; the cunning old farmer had withheld his permission until he knew the church would be willing to pay almost any price to have access to his field. I did not ask what price he had demanded, but then to ask parking fees as well . . .

"It's all cash too!" said Sergeant Bairstow. "He'll make a fortune today!"

"But he has saved us a lot of problems," said Father Summerson generously. "We must not be too harsh about him; after all, it is his field and I'm sure we must have incon-venienced him somewhat."

And so the day was a success. Craggs' field did accommodate most of the traffic and, as so often happens on these occasions, most of the vehicles were somehow parked before the service began. I went into the Mass and so did Sergeant Bairstow; it was a moving experience to see those ancient walls filled with people at prayer after so many centuries.

It would be some three weeks later when I saw Farmer Craggs again. He was crossing the market-place in Ashfordly and I hailed him.

"Thanks for helping us out that Sunday," I said.

"Ah's done meself a load of harm," he said, "lettin' yon field off like that."

"Harm?" I asked. "What sort of harm?"

"Somebody's told t' taxman about it, and now he's been through my money like a dose o' salts, checking this, checking that, counting egg money, taty money. Gahin back years, he is . . . Ah shall be worse off than ivver now . . ."

And he skulked away towards the bank.

I never did know who had informed the Inland Revenue about Mr Craggs, but it was not a very Christian thing to do.

CHAPTER 5

Tenants of life's middle state
Securely plac'd between the small and great.
WILLIAM COWPER, 1731—1800

While serving the rural community which comprised my
beat at Aidensfield, it dawned upon me that Crampton rarely
featured in my duty commitments. But I did not neglect
the village. I paid regular visits to its telephone kiosk during
my patrols and from time to time, performed traffic duty
outside the gates of the Manor. Whenever His Lordship and
Her Ladyship hosted one of their frequent and glittering
social functions, my role was to prevent people in smart
clothes and equally smart cars from interrupting the routine
of Crampton by indiscriminate parking. A car thoughtlessly
parked in a farm gateway can cause untold havoc and delay
in a rural timetable. Afterwards, I was usually invited into the
servants' quarters for a meal, an acceptable reward.

It was the ordinary people of Crampton who seldom
featured in my work. Apart from the occasional firearms certificate to renew or motoring offender to interview, there
was rarely anything of greater moment. No serious crimes
were committed; there were no domestic rows or breaches

of the peace of any kind. There was no council estate and no pub either; these facts might have been responsible for the happy absence of social problems, but this was not the entire answer. It appeared to me that the inhabitants of this peaceful place lived their quiet lives in an oasis of blissful contentment.

It was almost as if they lived on an island of ancient peace in the midst of a turbulent modern world. Without doubt, Crampton was different from many other villages, including those on my patch and elsewhere, but I could not immediately identify the subtle points of difference. By local standards, it was a medium-sized place of perhaps 300 inhabitants with a Methodist chapel and an Anglican parish church complete with a very scholarly vicar. There was a shop-cum-post office, a village school, several farms and many cottages, while prominent on the outskirts was the Manor.

These factors placed it squarely on the same basis as many local villages, while its pleasant situation overlooking the gentle and meandering River Rye gave it an added scenic dimension. It was a place of remarkable calm and beauty, one which was well off the proverbial beaten track and which therefore avoided the plague of tourism and the subsidiary diseases it left in its wake.

The entire village was constructed of mature local stone which grew more charming with the slow passage of time. The gentle tan shades of the stone; the careless patchwork of red pantile roofs interspaced by the occasional thatched cottage; the tiny well-kept gardens which glowed rich with colourful flowers from spring until autumn and the whispering trees in the surrounding parkland, all combined to provide Crampton with a serenity that was the envy of many. Its way of life echoed of centuries past.

The pace was so unhurried; the inhabitants were shy and retiring and even the schoolchildren went about their business in a quiet, well-ordered fashion. The handful of teenagers who lived in the village never caused me any concern and I often wondered how they spent their free time. They, and everyone else, seemed very content with their lot, but I felt they were not subdued in any way. As time went by, Crampton became an object of some fascination and even curiosity; I wondered what made it so different and why it existed in such a quiet but distinctive way.

The first clue came one Sunday.

It was 10.15 a.m. on a bright, sunny morning in April and I was standing outside the village telephone kiosk, making one of my points. I had hoisted my motorcycle on to its stand and it was leaning at an awkward angle with my crash helmet perched on the fuel tank. Its radio burbled incomprehensively in the peace of Crampton, but none of its messages were for me. This was the quiet scene as I waited in case the duty sergeant came to visit me, or in case someone from the office rang me on this public telephone.

All around, the birds were singing with the joys of spring and the village presented an idyllic picture of rustic calm. Its neat cottages nestled along each side of a trio of short streets; each of those streets clung to rising slopes of the valley as the morning sun glinted from their polished windows and fresh paintwork. Then I heard the sound of an expensive car engine.

Instinctively glancing in the direction of the noise, I saw a vintage Rolls-Royce emerge from the gates of Crampton Manor. It crawled sedately along the gravel road with uniformed chauffeur at the wheel, and I could see His Lordship and Her Ladyship in the rear seat. They were on their way to church. The splendid car, with every part shining after years of devoted care and constant polishing, cruised into the first street and stopped. The immaculately dressed Lord Crampton, a tall, slender man who oozed with the aristocratic breeding of his kind, climbed out and rapped on the door of a cottage with his silver-knobbed cane. Without waiting for a response, he moved to the adjoining cottage and repeated this action, then moved on to more cottages.

As he rapped successively on a sequence of doors, the car inched forward and then disappeared into Moor Street.

I left my place near the kiosk and hurried in that direction, ostensibly upon a short patrol but in reality fascinated by this behaviour. I was in time to see His Lordship rap on a further four doors, then he climbed into his car which cruised up the street, turned right at the top and vanished from view.

But now, Moor Street was alive with people dressed in their Sunday finery. From all the houses visited by His Lordship, there emerged families in their Sunday best, and as they trooped up the street towards the parish church on the hilltop, they in turn knocked on all the doors they passed. More people emerged and in seconds, Moor Street was filled with smart people of every age, all heading towards their parish church.

Now the Rolls-Royce was cruising down Dale Street and it halted at the top where a repeat performance was commenced. After His Lordship had rapped on four doors, the villagers emerged and knocked on others, and soon the populace of Dale Street was heading towards the church. As they walked and chattered happily, the Rolls turned into Middle Street which was where I happened to be. I had now returned to my kiosk and as the splendid vehicle turned towards me, Her Ladyship waved graciously and I responded with a polite salute, hatless though I was. I wondered if my action appeared to be the submissive touching of a forelock, but it was really a courteous acknowledgement.

The magnificent vehicle now stopped in this street. His Lordship, silver-topped cane in hand, thwacked more doors before ordering the car to continue. Off it went and by the time it halted at the lych-gate at the top of Middle Street, the entire Anglican population of Crampton, men, women and children, was marching towards the church. I've no idea how the Methodists, Catholics and other faiths fitted into this pattern and I did wonder, for just a fleeting moment, whether I was expected to attend. But I didn't make the gesture. I saw that His Lordship and Her Ladyship were first to enter the church, and noted that the early worshippers stood outside until the VIPs took their seats. Then everyone filed in. Only when the congregation was seated and the church full, did I hear the organist strike up the first hymn. It was precisely ten-thirty.

As I observed this quaint church-going arrangement, I realised I had witnessed a custom which had probably endured for centuries. I could imagine many past Lord Cramptons doing this self-same task from their ponies-and-traps, or from their coach-and-fours, and I now knew that I was working in a village whose ways had changed little since feudal times. The Rolls had replaced the horses; that was one visible sign of these modern times.

Few outsiders would be aware of this system of calling the faithful to church and I wondered whether the presence of individuals was monitored or checked in any way. Did His Lordship know when anyone had missed the service? And if so, what did he do? It was by pure chance that I had been in the village as this ritual was being executed, and it did give me a vital insight into the regulated mode of life in this charming, if somewhat old-fashioned village.

That Crampton continued to function along ancient feudal lines became more evident when I realised that the entire village was owned by Crampton Estate. It owned all the farms, the cottages and the shop; furthermore, most of the inhabitants worked on the estate. Some, however, were retired and continued to live in estate cottages for a meagre rent. I did learn, however, that one or two of the homes were now rented to younger village people who did not work for Crampton Estate, having secured work elsewhere. As time progressed, the number of estate workers was dwindling, but nonetheless, the estate had employed the parents and grand-parents of these younger people, so the link remained.

From that time, as I toured the village on my periodic patrols, I did notice that several of the smaller cottages were unoccupied and sadly noted that some were falling into der-eliction. Even if Crampton was clinging to its ancient ways, the Estate's power was being reduced simply because people were no longer working for it and occupying its cottages.

Sooner or later, these would be sold, I guessed, perhaps to be revived as second homes for wealthy outsiders, or even to be turned into holiday cottages by the Estate.

One such cottage was occupied by eighty-two-year-old Emily Finley, widow of the late Archie Finley who had been one of the Estate's carpenters. After Archie's death six years ago, Emily had continued to live in their beautiful little home for the tiniest of rents. She was well looked after by the Estate from both the financial and welfare point of view, a fact which made her old age and widowhood as happy as possible. Then Emily died, and I received a telephone call from the Estate Manager, Alan Ridley.

"It's Ridley at the Estate Office," said the voice one lunchtime. "You've probably heard that old Mrs Finley's died?"

"Yes." Word had reached me via the rural grapevine. "I had heard. There's no problem, is there?"

I was thinking in terms of the coroner and whether the death was in any way mysterious or suspicious; if so, I'd have to arrange a post-mortem, with all the resultant enquiries and maybe an inquest. A Sudden Death, as we termed this kind of happening, entailed a lot of police work.

"No, nothing like that, Mr Rhea. She died naturally, of old age I'd imagine. Her doctor's seen her and has issued the certificate. But it's her funeral on Wednesday in Crampton Parish Church. Eleven in the morning. The Estate is acting as undertaker. We do this for most of our employees and past employees and their spouses, free of charge, of course. There'll be a lot of cars and people about and we wondered if you would come along and keep an eye on things."

"Of course." I was only too pleased to oblige.

"I'd like to meet you on site to discuss the parking arrangements for the cortege, and of course, His Lordship's vehicle and those of the chief mourners."

And so I agreed. We fixed a date and time, and this aspect presented no real problems. We could utilise the village street for parking the cars of any incomers, while the church had adequate space to accommodate and park the funeral procession including the vehicles used by His Lordship and the official party. Most of the mourners, being residents of Crampton, would be on foot anyway, for it seemed that Emily had no close family — no children, brothers or sisters.

The body would remain in the cottage until the day of the funeral, unlike some villages where it would be taken into the church the previous night. It was scheduled to depart from Holly Cottage at ten minutes to eleven and to arrive at the church in time for the eleven o'clock commencement of the service. I decided to arrive at Crampton, in my best uniform and white gloves, by no later than ten-thirty.

Before embarking on this duty, I consulted Force Standing Orders to see if there was anything I should know about my conduct at a funeral. I learned that the only specific instruction said, "When passing a funeral cortege, members of the Force, of whatever rank, will salute the coffin."

Just before ten-thirty that Wednesday, therefore, I presented myself outside Emily Finley's cottage in the full knowledge that there would be little to do. But I did know that the presence of a uniformed police officer at a village funeral meant a great deal to the relatives of the deceased — for one thing, it added a touch of local stature to the final journey of the dear departed.

As I approached, I discovered that the entire population of the village had arrived outside Holly Cottage. Old and young alike were there, and I learned that the Estate had given all its workers the morning off so that they could attend the funeral. Dressed in their dark mourning clothes, the villagers congregated around the tiny house, spilling onto the road and across the smooth grass which fronted these pretty little homes. Due to the numbers, I did find myself having to keep them in some sort of order as several pressed forward and obstructed the route the coffin would take. It did mean, of course, that Mrs Finley was assured of a fine send-off. I felt she would have been surprised at the turnout, but on reflection accepted that this response was normal in this village.

Then the hearse arrived. But it wasn't a motor hearse, nor was it a horse-drawn vehicle. Some villages, I know, did make use of a black horse-drawn hearse with a smartly groomed black horse to draw it, but this was something entirely different. Between the ranks of assembled people, there appeared six young men smartly dressed in black suits, white shirts, black ties and bowler hats. I blinked as I saw them; they were all so like one another that they were difficult to tell apart. They resembled sextuplets, I thought, for they were like peas in the proverbial pod and they even moved in unison. In sombre silence, they were guiding something towards the cottage. It was a small four-wheeled trolley constructed of smart oak, with metal springs, spoked wheels and pneumatic tyres. Planks of oak formed two platforms, one above the other, the top one being about waist height. This polished and well-oiled vehicle, reminiscent of a pram without its cradle, moved silently and smoothly at the hands of its attendants. I noticed that Alan Ridley followed, now acting in his capacity as Estate undertaker. He was also clad in a black suit and bowler, and the little procession came to rest at the door of Mrs Finley's cottage.

Like everyone else, I stood in respectful silence to observe the proceedings and then the six men, preceded by Alan Ridley, moved indoors. They left the trolley outside. After a few minutes, the six emerged bearing the coffin on three strong slings which passed beneath it.

With obvious experience of similar small houses, they manoeuvred the coffin from the cramped space within and did so without dislodging the solitary wreath which lay on top. They hoisted the coffin onto the trolley, folded and stored the slings, then Alan Ridley approached with several more wreaths in his arms. These were carefully arranged on the lower level of the trolley hearse. When everything was in position, the funeral procession moved off. I walked ahead to halt any oncoming traffic that might arrive. To the sound of a tolling bell, the sombre procession filled the narrow confines of Middle Street as it climbed slowly towards the church; the six men did not have an easy task, guiding and pushing their precious load up the slope, but they succeeded.

They grew redder and redder in the face as the climb steepened and at the top, the vicar awaited beneath the lych-gate, the traditional resting place of corpses on their way to burial. His Lordship and Her Ladyship also waited at a discreet distance, standing close to the main door. Beneath the wooden cover of the lych-gate, the six bearers halted for just a moment to regain their breath and wipe the perspiration from their brows, and then the vicar began to recite the preliminary prayers. At this stage, the coffin, still on its wheels, was steered into the church. As it moved down the aisle, the accompanying mourners filed silently into their seats.

I saw Lord and Lady Crampton enter their pew as the coffin arrived at its position before the altar. I stayed at the back of the church.

At eleven o'clock prompt, the service began.

Even though I had never known Emily, I found both the service and the interment to be very moving. I gained the impression that the Estate and its workers were like a large and happy family; a true community which was being eradicated through the progress of time. Had Emily been buried by her few relatives, the church would not have been so full, nor would her funeral have been such an important event for the village. As things were, she was given a fitting farewell by those who knew and respected her. Following the interment, there was the traditional funeral lunch of ham in the Tenants' Room at the Hall. Everyone was invited, including myself.

There, I was privately thanked by Alan Ridley for the small part I had played, and I learned that the six bearers were three brothers and their three cousins. They all worked on the Estate as carpenters, stone masons, electricians and plumbers. Acting as bearers during Estate funerals was one of their regular additional commitments.

As I motorcycled home afterwards, I realised why this village did not feature greatly in any of my crime returns or in the Divisional Offence Report Register. It was due,

I felt, to the family atmosphere of Crampton and the close relationship between everyone who lived and worked here. That closeness affected both their working and private lives.

I had no doubt that if a small crime did occur, a theft for example, it would be dealt with locally and I would never know about it. Perhaps the threat of dismissal from employment by the Estate caused everyone to be law-abiding, and I did know that the Estate dealt with any local disputes between neighbours. There were no domestic disputes in Crampton of the kind that officially concerned me, but I knew that this feudal type of existence was drawing to a close. And with its decline would come social problems and community strife.

As the deserted cottages were sold and occupied by outsiders, so this enduring family atmosphere would be diluted and the problems and difficulties of the outside world would afflict the village. The Estate would lose its paternal control for better or for worse, and I wondered if this would happen during my period as the village constable. After all, we were in the second half of the twentieth century, but it was pleasing to know that this kind of contented and untroubled life did continue in part of the English countryside.

But there was one occasion when I had to deal with a small outbreak of trouble in Crampton. Curiously, it arose as an indirect result of Emily Finley's death. Perhaps, to be more precise, it arose because of her empty cottage, but it did mean that I had to take out my notebook and begin the steps necessary to institute criminal proceedings.

To set the scene, it became the policy of Crampton Estate to sell off those empty cottages for which they had no foreseeable use. This applied especially to those which required a lot of renovation and modernization. As cottages became vacant, in the way that Emily's did, the Estate had to decide whether they were required for new workers, married staff, larger or smaller families or retiring employees. The work force was contracting; it was happening everywhere in the countryside and fewer cottages were needed.

Nonetheless, Crampton Estate did occasionally take on new workers from outside.

Some of them required a house, and Emily's cottage had become vacant at the very time the Estate was considering the appointment of a trained accountant. Its increasingly complicated book-keeping now required those kinds of skills and so Emily's little house was earmarked as a possible home for this new member of staff. Over the weeks following her death, I noticed that the house had been renovated. Scaffolding appeared outside and pointing of the stonework was undertaken. New tiles were fitted to the roof and piles of stones, bricks and cement appeared in the garden as internal structural changes were made. A new bath was fitted and the kitchen was brought up to the standards of the period; the house was re-wired too and a partial damp-course installed.

Around this time, one day in May, I had to visit the Estate Office about some cattle movement licences and was offered a coffee by Alan Ridley.

"I see Mrs Finley's cottage is nearly finished," I said after we had concluded our official business.

"Give it another week," he said. "It looks nice now. I wish she could have seen it, the work was long overdue. But we can't do that kind of job with folks living in them. Besides, old folks don't like upheaval or changes to their homes."

"You've appointed an accountant, I hear?" I put to him.

"Yes, a woman. A Miss Rogers. Jean Rogers. She starts a week on Monday."

"And she'll occupy that little house?" I was updating my local knowledge of the village.

Alan laughed. "In theory, yes. In practice, no. You know," he added almost as an afterthought, "I think you ought to be in Crampton a week on Monday, say from eight o'clock in the morning."

"Really, why?" I asked, slightly puzzled.

"That's the day we hand over the keys to Mrs Finley's cottage," he said, and I detected a distinct twinkle in his eye. "But we give them to the Maintenance Foreman; he arranges the housing moves. Might I suggest you are outside Mrs Finley's house just before eight?"

"You won't be expecting trouble, will you?" I asked, wondering what lay behind his suggestion.

"No," he said, "but I think you'll find it an interesting experience."

So I arranged my duties to accommodate this unusual suggestion and on that Monday morning, I decided to perform one of my rare foot patrols around Crampton. I began at seven-thirty and enjoyed the morning stroll; the village was full of rich blossom and in places, the clean, crisp air was heavy with varied scents. Birds were singing and the morning was dewy and bright, with the sun gaining in strength as it rose in the sky. It was a moment from a corner of heaven.

Just before eight o'clock, I made my way around to Middle Street, towards Mrs Finley's cottage, as everyone called it. Few people referred to it as Holly Cottage. I was surprised to see that a small crowd had gathered. It comprised men, women and children and I must admit that this baffled me. The sight made me wonder what was about to happen and why I was really here.

Then Alan Ridley arrived on foot. He acknowledged my presence with a brief nod and stood before the front door of the cottage, awaiting eight o'clock. As the church clock struck the hour, the Maintenance Foreman, a dour Yorkshireman called Charlie Atkinson, came forward. He was dressed in his overalls and ready for work.

As the clock was striking, Alan handed over to him the two keys of Mrs Finley's cottage, one for the back door and one for the front.

Charlie then called, "Sidney and Alice Brent!"

A man came forward and accepted the keys. At the same time, Sidney Brent handed some keys to Charlie who announced, "George and Ann Clifton."

The Cliftons came forward, accepted the Brent keys, and then passed up some of their own.

"Alex Cooper," and an elderly man emerged from the crowd to accept the Cliftons' keys. He handed some back to Charlie, and so the process continued with about twelve families waiting to hand over their keys and accept others in return.

During this short ceremony, Alan Ridley moved to my side.

"Well?" he asked quizzically. "Have you got it worked out?"

"No," I admitted. "What's going on?"

"We're re-housing," he smiled. "Or, to be exact, our tenants are re-housing themselves."

"All these?"

He nodded; already, those who had been first in the queue, were disappearing hurriedly towards their homes.

"All of them," he said. "In a few minutes, all hell will break loose. The Brents will be coming here, to occupy Mrs Finley's cottage, and they'll want to be in right away. But that's Charlie's problem. Come along, let's go."

He began to walk along the village towards his own office in the Hall and I fell into step at his side.

"So what's going on?" I asked as we distanced ourselves from the gathering.

"It's an old practice on this Estate," he adopted a serious voice. "When we appoint someone to our staff, we offer to house them. It happens everywhere — tied cottages, you know. And so we select one of our empty houses and modernize it. We clean and decorate it, as we did with Mrs Finley's."

"But all those people handing in keys . . ." I began.

"Yes," he said. "At some time in the past, long before my arrival here, this kind of thing caused an upset in the village. In appointing and housing newcomers in refurbished homes, we created the situation where workers of long standing were living in properties which were below the standard we offered to the newcomers. The newcomer's home was always refurbished and modernized, in the way you've just seen. So the tenants decided that whenever a house became vacant and was modernized, the longest serving tenant should move in, if he or she wanted to."

I realised how things worked.

"So they all move up a notch?" I put to him.

"Yes, the whole village waits for an empty house like this. On the day, they're packed and ready, and so, in a few minutes, the Brents will move into Mrs Finley's nice cottage, and then the Cliftons will move into the Brents', old Alex Cooper will move into the Cliftons' . . ."

"And your new accountant? Where does she fit into all this?" I asked.

"It's not going to be easy, with her coming from outside the village. I'll have to explain things to her. To be honest, some of our manual workers, especially those from here, are quite happy to accept a cottage which is, to be truthful, at the bottom of our heap. In the past, they did so because they desperately needed accommodation, and the rents we charged were affordable to the poorest. But low rents meant we hadn't the funds to modernize the homes. For a pepper-corn rent, those folks were happy to live in less-than-perfect accommodation. Their "carrot" was to wait for the kind of movement you've seen today. It enabled them to move up the scale and, let's face it, the Estate benefits because it needs to modernize only one house every few years. It saves us money and keeps rent down. Eventually, everyone should get a chance to occupy such a place. But I fear our new lady worker will not tolerate a house which is the last of today's line — it's grotty, to say the least. We may sell it. She has hinted she might buy a house locally. If we appoint more people from outside, then our system of moving tenants is likely to die out, I feel."

"A strange system," I commented.

"Now, if you go back into the village, you'll see that there is a flurry of activity, with well over a dozen families moving house. They're all moving today and all before ten o'clock!"

"You impose a deadline?"

"We must. Officially, they're not supposed to do it, but we close our eyes and go along with the idea, up to a point. That's why Charlie handles all the keys — it keeps some sort of order, and it makes the tenants think it's got our formal blessing. So we give them time off between eight and ten to make their moves."

When I walked back through Crampton, an amazing sight met my eyes. The village seemed full of carts, cars, lorries and anything that would transport furniture. Already, many items were on board — three-piece suites, wardrobes, beds and tea-chests full of crockery. The gardens and grassy areas outside the cottages were covered with household belongings and people were rushing in and out with arms full of objects. Helpers were flinging things on to the vehicles and it seemed there was a race to be first into another home. It was an amazing sight, a community house removal of the like I've never seen before nor since.

As I strolled about to observe this peculiar occurrence, I came across an argument, a rare event in Crampton. From a distance, I knew some kind of dispute was raging and that it involved a pile of furniture on a horse-drawn cart. The air was full of ripe language while angry arms were waving between the protagonists. Then one of them spotted me.

"Here's t' bobby," I heard. "Ask him!"

One of the men hailed me and I strode across.

"Yes?" I asked of anyone who might answer. There were eight or nine people standing around the loaded cart. It was one of the old so-called market carts, a tipper with two wheels and a tailboard which lowered to facilitate loading and unloading. Already, it looked precariously overloaded with a tall wardrobe standing upright and a chest of drawers hanging over the tailboard. Every spare piece of space was filled with domestic odds and ends.

"Mr Rhea," the man holding the horse's head addressed me. I knew him by sight but did not know his name. "Settle this for us, wilt thoo?"

They all began to shout at once, and I appealed for calm, then addressed the man with the horse.

"Ah 'm t' owner of this cart," he said, "and Ah live out near t' bridge, on t' road to Brantsford. Hawkins is the name."

"Go on," I invited.

"This chap 'ere," and he pointed to a young man close to the tail of the cart, "well, 'e asked me to help him shift this stuff today. Hired me 'orse and cart to 'im, Ah did. Half a crown an hour."

"Is this right?" I asked the man lurking at the tail.

He nodded, with a sly grin on his face, as the cart-owner continued.

"Two jobs to do," he said, "his mum and dad out of this house here, and into that 'un there," and he pointed to a pair of houses almost opposite one another. "Then, after that, Ah was asked to shift him and his missus and kids out of his spot and into that 'n what was occupied by his mum and dad."

"Yes," I followed it so far. Mum and dad into a smaller house, and son and growing family into their old house, which was slightly larger. Very sensible.

"Well," said the cart man, "him and his mates, all his brothers and what-have-you loaded me up with his dad and mum's furniture for t' first job and got me unloaded, all in seven minutes. Seven minutes to move house! When Ah got loaded up for t' second trip, from his house to his mum's spot, he said they'd do t' same all over again, load and unload in another seven minutes."

"So?" I had not yet discovered the cause of the dispute.

"Well, they're saying that because Ah charges half a crown an hour, and it hasn't taken an hour, then they don't have to pay!"

"Did you tell them that the half-crown was the minimum charge for an hour or part of an hour?" I asked him.

"Nay, Ah didn't! There's no need for that sort of carry-on, Mr Rhea. Damn it, Ah thought two house jobs would take all morning, not fourteen minutes . . ."

This was not a police matter. It was what we called a business dispute, and so I told him that. I said it was nothing to do with the police; it was purely a business disagreement which must be sorted out between themselves.

"Then Ah shall keep this stuff on t' cart until t' hour's up," he said, "then Ah'll be in my rights to ask for t' money."

"We'll unload it," said the young man to his brothers and family. "Howway, lads, get cracking. We can beat our last record for unloading, I reckon . . ."

But Hawkins had a different idea.

"Nay!" he shouted. "Thoo can't touch this stuff! Not yet," and he rapped the horse's flanks with a rein. It moved off quickly, but everyone followed, trying to grab items and carry them indoors. Some of the smaller stuff was lifted off, but the larger items were impossible to move. As the horse broke into a trot, its intrepid owner ran alongside and then jumped on to the front edge of his cart where the shafts met the body, and he sat there, reins in hand, as he whipped the horse into a gallop.

The furniture bounced and jolted along the street as the horse and cart left the family behind and then Hawkins halted. In a flash, he jumped off his cart and loosened the primitive tipping mechanism. With a jangling of metal, the bolts fell free and he slapped the horse.

It moved a short distance and the cart, now unbalanced, tipped backwards as all the furniture slid off the back and spread across the road. In a long, untidy line, furniture, clothes, pots and pans, clip rugs and a motley collection of things rolled into the street.

"If you're not paying, then Ah 'm not moving it," said Hawkins, folding his arms to observe the mayhem. At the moment the family ran towards their scattered belongings, a service bus, followed by an oil tanker, turned into the street. And at that same moment, I knew I had before me a clear case of 'Obstruction of the Highway'. The bus driver started to shout at Hawkins, but he only laughed as he managed to secure his cart to its chassis during the fuss. All this was happening as I approached the scene in the ponderous strides of the constabulary in action. Hawkins, however, was quickly mobile and trotted away his horse, chortling at his own astuteness.

"You'll have to move this stuff!" I ordered the owners. "It's obstructing the road."

"Not us!" snapped the brothers. "Hawkins dumped it, Hawkins can shift it!"

"You'll all get fined for obstructing this road," I shouted above the din. "And it'll be far more than the cost of hiring that cart!"

"Nope," said the family. "It stays."

Hawkins was already some distance away, and I would have to report him too; I knew where he lived.

The tanker driver leaned out of his cab. "Are they going to shift that rubbish or shall I drive over it?" he shouted above the noise.

A stout, middle-aged woman wielding a broom came running to the scene, crying and saying, "Our Harry, you stupid oaf! Get it shifted, now," and she started to belabour him with the broom handle. Confronted by such positive persuasion, Harry and the other men of the family soon cleared a road through for the bus and the tanker, and then, as the heat of the moment evaporated, they began to man-handle their stuff to the side of the road. It took much longer than seven minutes.

So far as I know Hawkins never received any payment for that task, but he did eventually receive a summons after I had reported both him and the key members of that large family for 'Obstruction of the Highway'. When the Superintendent read my report, he laughed and formally cautioned each party, so there was no court case.

Never again was I involved in the house-moving customs of Crampton, and sometimes I wonder if they still continue. And I'm also curious as to whether anyone has broken the Crampton record of seven minutes for moving the contents of one house into another.

CHAPTER 6

The love of money is the root of all evil.
ST PAUL, d. *circa* AD 67

One of the less publicised aspects of constabulary work is the quiet assistance that police officers give to members of the public; it would be possible to fill a book with glowing examples. This help comes in many forms, such as assisting in the repair of a broken-down car; catching stray budgies; helping with the formalities of bureaucracy or coaxing worried souls through the maze of complex problems that life throws at them.

I recall one example which involved a colleague of mine. He was performing night duty on a main trunk road and came upon a family car which had broken down. It was a major defect and there was no overnight garage in the area. He learned that the occupants were heading for London; driving through the night to catch a morning flight for a long-overdue visit to an aged relative in Australia. Marooned as they were in the middle of the North Riding of Yorkshire, the constable promptly ended his shift by taking some time off duty. He was able to do this because of some overtime previously worked, and with no thought of being paid or even thanked, he drove the stranded family to London in his own car. It was a distance of 250 miles each way and they caught their flight.

Countless minor tasks are completed during a police officer's daily round, each in itself a small thing, albeit of great value to the person who is helped. One feature of this work is that it provides a vivid insight into the private lives of others.

One example which occurred on my patch at Aidensfield involved Awd Eustace, whose real name was Eustace Wakefield.

His problem was that he could not light his fire, a fact which came to my notice early one winter morning. The house next door to his was empty for three months while the owners were overseas, and I was keeping an eye on it. This meant regular visits to ensure it hadn't been broken into or vandalised, and it was while examining the rear of this house that I noticed Eustace. He was chopping sticks just over the separating fence, so I said, "Good morning."

"Morning." He was a slight man with long, unkempt grey hair and stooped with age. Ragged old clothes, over which he wore a tattered cardigan, attempted to protect him against the icy winds of winter and he wore woollen gloves without any fingers. He was hacking away at some small logs and chopping them into kindling sticks.

"That'll warm you up," I said, mindful of the Yorkshire notion that the act of chopping sticks warms you twice — once when chopping them and again when blazing on a fire.

"It would if Ah could get that bloody fire o' mine going," said the little fellow. "Damned thing, it won't draw. Them sticks is wet, mebbe."

"They look OK to me," I peered across the fence to examine them.

"Ah've tried and tried this morning," he said. "Damn thing won't blaze so Ah can't even boil me kettle."

"I'll come round," I heard myself make an offer of help.

There was no wonder his fire wouldn't ignite. It stood no chance. His grate was part of an old range of the Yorkist type. It had an oven at one side and a centrally positioned black leaded grate some two feet above floor level. At the opposite side of the oven was a hot water tank; this was built into the fireplace and fitted with a brass tap to draw off the heated water. A small can with a wire handle hung from that tap, and a kettle of cold water waited on a swivel hob.

But the grate was overflowing with ash. It was inches deep within the grate itself, but the tall space below was also full. The ash spilled and spread for a distance of about a yard into the dusty room. Directly on top of all this, he had tried to light his pathetic fire; the evidence was there in the form of charred newspapers and sticks, with odd lumps of coal uselessly placed.

"It'll never go with all that muck underneath," I kicked the accumulated ash with my boot. "It needs cleaning out, you need a draught for a fire to blaze. You've choked it to death!"

"Oh," he said as if not fully understanding this elementary fact.

"Where's your shovel?" I asked and he produced a battered one from its place near the sink. I began to scoop shovelfuls from the huge pile of ash and soon had enough to fill his dustbin. After a few minutes of this dusty, hectic work, during which I removed my tunic and cap, I had his fireplace cleaned out and had added a layer of thick dust to that which coated all his belongings.

"Right," I said. "Paper and sticks next."

He had a store of old newspapers in a wall cupboard and brought in some of the sticks he had been chopping.

"You ought to get some more chopped," I suggested, "and put them in this side oven to dry. But these aren't bad, they're dry enough."

I laid his fire then went out to his coal-house. But it was almost bare. In one dark corner were a few lumps of coal, scarcely enough to last out the day. I managed to scrape sufficient for my task and laid it on the fire, applied a match and very soon it was blazing merrily.

"I'll tell the coalman to call," I said to Eustace, taking his kettle and weighing it in my hands to see if it was full. It was, so I turned the swivel hob over the blaze so that the kettle would boil for his pot of tea. "You're nearly out, you'll need some today."

"Ah've no money," he said. "Ah've no money for coal . . ."

"Your pension's due on Thursday, isn't it?"

"Aye, well, t' coalman might wait a day or two then." As I stood before the welcoming blaze, I was well aware that this old man was poverty-stricken. The tiny back room, which served as lounge, living-room and kitchen, was dismal and virtually bare. The only furnishings were an old armchair with the stuffing protruding, a battered table and one old kitchen chair. There was a small, well-worn clip rug before the fire, but the stone floor was otherwise bare and in one corner there was a large brown earthenware sink with a cold-water tap. The wooden draining-board contained all his crockery; it had been washed and stacked there until required. The bare walls had been distempered years ago and never cleaned or papered since.

The toilet, which was a WC, was outside next to the coal shed and there was another room downstairs, but I did not go in, nor did I venture upstairs. It was plain to see that Awd Eustace lived in desperately poor accommodation with no money to spend on luxuries or even the basic necessities of life. I felt sorry for him and promised to look in from time to time.

When I left, he seemed happier and the kettle was beginning to sing. Later in the day, I came across the coalman as he was making some deliveries in Elsinby and asked him to drop a few sacks into Awd Eustace's shed. This he promised to do. I explained about Eustace's pension and the coalman was quite happy to wait for his payment.

From that time onwards, I made a practice of popping in to see old Eustace, but he never improved his ways. He never cleaned out his grate and always had trouble getting a fire going, so I became his regular grate-cleaner. Sometimes, I would stay and sample a cup of weak tea but he seldom chatted about himself. I did learn, however, that he had no family, except for a brother who lived somewhere in the Birmingham area. They'd not communicated for years. To earn a living, Eustace had worked on local farms all his life, labouring and doing odd jobs. He'd retired about twelve years ago and had come to spend his final years in this tiny house.

Then one day I called and there was no sign of him. A bottle of milk stood on the doorstep and immediately I feared the worst. I knocked several times, then forced my way in and found him dead in bed. It is unnecessary to dwell upon the formalities that followed, except to say that he died of natural causes. A few days later, a solicitor contacted me. He asked me to be present as he searched Eustace's home for personal effects and documents. And the result was astounding.

We found twelve Building Society passbooks, each containing the maximum deposit of £5000; there were bags of bank notes under the bed and stuffed in his cupboards; a sack half full of gold sovereigns, and share certificates galore filed neatly in a battered suitcase. For a police constable, whose salary was then about £650 per annum, this was a fortune. The wealth in this hovel was staggering.

Awd Eustace had left a fortune and I expected it would go to his brother. Eustace had always existed on the smallest amount of money; putting all his savings away in stocks and shares, and in the building societies. The house was his own too, and so he could have lived a very comfortable and happy life. Why he chose to live in such lowly conditions, I do not know but there were many like him.

One old character always sat and read by the light of a candle, and once when I called to see if he was all right, he welcomed me into his room, settled me in a chair, and then blew out the candle.

"Thoo dissn't need flight of a candle just ti chat," he said, as if in explanation. "There's neea point in wasting good money." And I learned later that the same old man, who'd been left a lot of valuables by his well-to-do father, was quite content to barter a silk tie in return for a cabbage, or an exquisite piece of china for a few eggs. It was rumoured he could be seen in the light of his candle as he counted his piles of money, but I never witnessed this.

There were many similar instances of Yorkshire canniness in the handling of money; it has often been said that if a coin fell over the side of a ship with a Scotsman and a Yorkshireman on board, the Yorkshireman would be first into the water to retrieve it. There is no doubt that some Yorkshire folk are very careful and this trait was noticeable among police officers and their wives.

There were, and still are, some very tight-fisted policemen and some equally careful wives. It must be said that the policeman's wage at that time was very poor and those with growing families did find it difficult to manage, myself included. Many made skilful economies but some went to extreme odds. I knew one lady who bought an electric washing-machine after months of careful saving, and then, in order to use it, sat up until after midnight so she could take advantage of cheap electricity. The burning lights probably cost more than she saved — unless she worked in the dark.

Another had a similar line of thought. Her parents bought her a washing-up machine, a fine piece of equipment which washed all her pots. But the woman worried about the cost of running it; the thought of massive electricity bills so horrified her that she decided to run it during the night. In this way, the cheaper electricity could be utilised to the full and the machine would be used only when it was completely full of dirty pots.

The snag was that the family had only one set of crockery. When all the pieces were dirty, they were placed into the machine and the family had to wait until next morning before they could be re-used. The mother would not hear of the machine being used during the daytime, so she bought a second set of crockery. But as one set was used at breakfast, another at lunch and some pieces casually during the day, two sets were not enough. So she bought a third set, with a few spare mugs and plates . . .

The result was that during the night hours, her washing-up machine, filled with three full sets of crockery from breakfast, lunch and tea, rumbled along on its cheap power. I don't know what it cost her in spare crockery and I often wonder if she thought she was being economical.

Inevitably, with circulating tales of such tightfistedness, (a state of mind which is very often regarded as common sense by its perpetrators) there are discussions as to which person, within our knowledge, is the meanest. All men know the fellow who will never buy his round in a pub; who coasts downhill in his car to save petrol or who always uses the office telephone to make his calls. Invariably, though, there is one person who becomes a legend in his own lifetime so far as tightfistedness is concerned. The police service is just as prone as any other profession and in our case, such a man was Police Constable Meredith Dryden.

Of middle service and approaching his forties, he sported a ruddy, moon-shaped face and a nice head of dark, curly hair. He'd been reared in a village on the Yorkshire Wolds and was as careful as any man I know. He did free-wheel his private car down hills to save petrol, and did switch his house lights off each time he left a room, even for five minutes: what he saved on electricity was spent on replacing baffled bulbs. He grew his own vegetables which he sold to his wife at market prices; made all his family use the same bathwater to save on heating costs, and even cut his own hair.

When he first came to my notice, he was stationed on the coast, but was later transferred to Brantsford, just along the road from Aidensfield and Ashfordly. His reputation preceded him; long before Meredith arrived, we heard about his legendary meanness and wondered how he would get along with the happy-go-lucky members of Ashfordly section.

One of his habits quickly manifested itself. He got others to run errands for him on the grounds that it both saved his boot leather and obviated a lot of the aggravation that followed his miserly actions. I came across this one day when I was in the tiny police office of Brantsford. Meredith was sitting at the typewriter and a young probationer constable was at his side.

As I entered, midway through one of my motorcycle patrols, Meredith said to the youngster, "Paul, nip down to the newsagents, will you? Get me a copy of the *Yorkshire Post* — I can read it over my coffee break."

Eager to please, the lad put on his cap and off he went; I made some coffee as Meredith worked, and by the time the kettle had boiled, Paul had returned with the newspaper.

"Thanks," said Meredith, not offering any payment to the youngster. We chatted over our coffee, and Meredith scanned the newspaper. Then, when we'd finished, he handed it back to the lad.

"Thanks, take it back to the shop. Tell 'em I'd gone when you got back."

And so the young policeman was faced with the embarrassing choice of either taking back the paper, or keeping it himself. He kept it, but he learned not to run any more errands for Meredith the Miser, as we named him. In the office, he collected bits of string and old envelopes for use at home and on one occasion when a lady came collecting for the Red Cross, Meredith slipped a threepenny bit into her box, and then made an entry in his official notebook to the effect that he had done so. This was complete with the date, time and place of the transaction.

"You never know when folks are on the fiddle," he said earnestly. "I'll check that the money has gone to the right place, just to be sure." And he did.

We had heard that Meredith used his tea-bags several times before throwing them out and that he made his wife wait until the shops were on the point of closing before entering to make her purchases of perishable goods. That way, she often got the tail-end bargains of the day, such as cheap fruit and vegetables, or damaged tins of stuff. On the topic of housekeeping, word had reached us that his wife, Ruth, had to make a weekly request for the precise amount of cash she needed, whereupon Meredith would draw the cash from the bank.

Just how precisely his mind operated was revealed to me one Friday morning. On another of my motorcycle routes, I popped into Brantsford Police Station with some reports for signature, and Meredith was there.

I brewed some coffee and brought two cups into the front office. We sat and talked for a few minutes about our work, then I stood up and said, "Well, Meredith, I must be off. I've work to do and people to see."

"That'll be tuppence," he said, "for the coffee."

"No," I tried to correct him, "we pay into a fund for the coffee, both here and at Ashfordly. Sergeant Bairstow collects it — I'm up to date with my payments."

"I know, but we ran out of office coffee. This is my own — I brought it in for today, for myself. You owe me for one cup and some milk. Tuppence."

For a moment, I thought he was joking, but the expression on that florid face told me he was serious. I handed over two pennies.

"Going far?" he asked, as I replaced my crash helmet, still smarting from his actions.

"Briggsby eventually," I said, "and then Thackerston."

"You couldn't do a job for me, could you?" The request was pleasant enough. From an ordinary person, there would have been an instant and positive response, but as this was coming from Meredith the Miser, I had to consider all the likely consequences.

"What sort of a job?" I was wary of the things he had asked others to do.

"Cash a cheque for me at the bank before you leave town?"

After a moment's reflection, I agreed. I needed to cash one of my own for housekeeping, and so it would not be a hindrance. Meredith gave me a cheque for £6 13s 2d, and I said I would be happy to cash it.

It transpired that this was for his wife's housekeeping that week. I had no problem cashing it for him, but I now realised that it was true that Meredith did calculate the week's housekeeping allowance literally down to the last penny. Furthermore, he regularly went shopping with her when his duties permitted, his purpose being to ensure that she bought the cheapest goods without exceeding the tight budget he imposed. If possible, she had to save from her allowance. We began to feel sorry for poor Ruth Dryden.

Then Meredith had an apparent flush of generosity because he invited Alwyn Foxton and his wife for a day's outing on the moors. Alwyn had been at training-school with Meredith and was perhaps his closest companion.

"It's my birthday on Sunday," Meredith had told him. "I'm forty. Life begins at forty, so they say. I thought you and Betty, and me and Ruth, could have a day out on the moors to celebrate. I'm off duty that day. We'll use my car and we'll stop and have lunch at a pub, and then take things as they come."

I do know that Alwyn was surprised by this invitation, as indeed everyone was, and he agreed to go on the outing. For the rest of us, as mere onlookers, it did seem that Meredith had mellowed and that the onset of forty had opened his mind and his wallet.

The historic outing was scheduled for the second Sunday in May and I recall that it was a beautiful day with clear skies and bright sunshine. The countryside was at its best, with fresh, new greenery along the hedgerows, colourful flowers in abundance both in the wild and in the rustic gardens, and a barrage of birdsong to complete the idyllic picture. The outing should be wonderful; I wished I was going (albeit not with Meredith), but I was performing a local duty that day.

It would be about a week afterwards when I next saw Alwyn, his grey hair perhaps a few shades whiter and his face drawn with anger. He had an envelope in his hand.

"Are you all right, Alwyn?" I asked. At that moment, I had forgotten all about the moorland outing and was concerned for his health. He did look pale and sick, and I had a feeling it was connected with the letter in his hand.

"No I am not!" he fumed. "The bloody man!"

I did not know what to say or how to react, but he said, "You know that bloody man Meredith the Miser?"

"Yes," I said tentatively.

"You were there, weren't you? When he invited me and Betty to have a day out with him? It was his birthday."

"Yes," I acknowledged. "How did it go?"

"It cost me a bloody fortune!" Alwyn snapped, sitting down at the desk. "Meredith turned up in his car, as promised, and in we jumped. We went up to Rosedale and Hutton-le-Hole and after a walk we all went to a cafe for some morning coffee."

"That was nice of him," I commented for want of something better to say.

"Nothing of the sort!" snapped Alwyn. "By the time the bill came, he managed to disappear into the toilet. I paid, and I was happy to do so at the time. At that point, there was nothing to grumble about."

It was evident that Meredith had been on top form that day, and so I settled down to hear more from Alwyn.

"We drove all over, stopping in villages, pausing to look at views and that sort of thing. In fact, Nick, it was a lovely outing. The moors were splendid and there's some magnificent scenery off the beaten track. Then we stopped at a pub which served bar snacks for lunch. Well, I paid for the first round of drinks and when the time came for the second, he went to make a telephone call. I paid for that round as well. Then Meredith told the landlord it was his birthday and ordered wine, and we had a smashing meal. And would you believe it, when the landlord brought the bill, Meredith vanished into the toilet again."

"He did you again!" I grinned.

"Yes, I paid. I thought he'd square up with me later, so I paid up. I didn't want to cause any embarrassment in the pub. I thought he'd go halves at least, but he never offered a penny. Not a bloody penny! He just jumped into his car and came home, and thanked me for a lovely day out. I hadn't the heart to demand half-shares from him, not on his birthday."

"Alwyn, old son," I said, "you know what the fellow's like, we all know what he's like. You should have been wary of him — and now you've given him a birthday treat, haven't you. I reckon he spends hours planning these campaigns."

"That's not all." Alwyn held up the envelope which had so clearly upset him. "Seen this?" and he passed it to me.

It was a bill from Meredith. He was asking Alwyn to pay for half the petrol used on that outing.

In spite of our knowledge of Meredith and his methods, he continued to score against us in our off-guarded moments. At one time or another, most of us found ourselves at the expensive end of Meredith's guile. He managed on one occasion to get me to buy two raffle tickets for him; as the seller waited for Meredith to finish a telephone call, I paid her, but he never paid me. I don't think he won a prize but nor did I.

Then it was time for duty at York Races. The May meeting is always so pleasant, for the course is at its floral best and every one of us wanted to be selected as additional strength to aid York City Police. Extra officers were drafted in from all the neighbouring forces for duty at this busy course on race days. Such duties came around only once in a while, and it was so nice to be nominated. When I looked at the names of the colleagues who were to accompany me, I saw that Meredith was one of them. I made a vow to keep out of his way where money was involved.

In those days, we travelled by train and had to lodge overnight in York for the duration of the three-day meeting. Our digs were in some old terraced houses which overlooked the racecourse and for each of the three days we paraded at 11 a.m. for our duties. They included car-parking; security of the track, the horses and the jockeys; plus a watch for pickpockets, car thieves and the other unsavoury characters who prey on their fellows at race meetings, with a general brief to ensure that things progressed smoothly. It was a hard, but pleasant three days and we usually finished duty around six o'clock following dispersal of traffic after the last race. During our two evenings in digs, we went either to the cinema or to the local pubs for a drink or two, but if we were broke, we stayed in and played cards or dominoes.

Although we were not allowed to place bets while in uniform, we did manage to persuade CID officers or other acquaintances to put money on our selections. We enjoyed race meetings; they were a real tonic and a break from our more mundane duties.

Throughout that May meeting, Meredith's miserly reputation caused him to be frozen out of many social events; if drinks were bought, he was ignored unless he could be forced into buying a round. And that was a rare event. He was not allowed to play darts, dominoes or cards unless he put his money on the table first and in this cruel way the men, all of us, kept him at bay. Our actions did not make him alter his attitude; he remained as tight-fisted and miserly as ever, and after the final day, as we travelled home by train, this character-trait shone through more strongly than ever.

Our train journey took us to Eltering where an official car would be waiting to take us home. The trip from York was through some delightful countryside but we were too tired and too broke to appreciate it; exhausted, broke and hungry, we were concerned only with getting home.

None of us had any money left; we'd either lost it on the horses or spent it on our enjoyment at the pubs or pictures, and so that long journey was pretty miserable. There were no refreshment cars on a trip of that kind — besides, none of us could have found the necessary cash to buy anything. There were eight of us in our carriage, all sitting quietly as we brooded over the past three days. Meredith was one and he was just as quiet as the others.

As the train chugged along, someone would say, "By, I could just eat a round of fish and chips!" or "I could do with a drink," or "I'm famished . . . oh, for summat to eat . . ." But no one had anything to offer. We were skint.

And then, on the final miles into Eltering, our train entered a tunnel; it was about half a mile long, and in those days, the trains did not have lights on for such short trips in the darkness. We all sat there in silence, and when we emerged, Meredith was eating a toffee.

"Meredith, you sneaking sod!" snapped one of the men.

"Well, I did pass them around," he said, chewing contentedly.

He made no offer to pass them around again, and from that point, I believed the story that Meredith could and indeed would peel an orange one-handed while it was in his pocket.

But with tales of such behaviour circulating among a group of men like police officers, it was inevitable that they would make some effort to teach Meredith a lesson.

I'm not sure how or where the notion originated, or indeed who was the instigator, but gradually there arose a group feeling that Meredith was due to receive some kind of comeuppance, preferably of a financial nature. He had to be forced to pay for all his past transgressions, and we knew that this would be one of our most difficult achievements. Getting Meredith to pay for anything was rather like trying to climb Everest in a swimsuit.

As this germ of an idea floated around, it produced some good suggestions and some improbable ones; and it was by coincidence that Sergeant Bairstow said there ought to be a get-together for all members of the section. He proposed dinner at a local inn, one to which we could take our wives and meet one another socially and at leisure over a meal and a drink. Getting policemen together like this was nigh impossible due to their varied shifts and periods off duty, and even a determined effort like this would mean that someone was left out. We decided that special constables would man the market towns that evening so that the maximum attendance was assured.

Basically, it was a good idea. As the notion began to gain substance, it dawned upon us that this was the ideal opportunity to get our revenge on Meredith. We counted the likely numbers who would attend, and included our two sergeants, Charlie Bairstow and Oscar Blaketon. It was important that we discreetly tempted Meredith to attend; getting him there at all would be a difficult task because it meant he must be willing to pay his share. So we decided to invite the Inspector. Almost imperceptibly, the purpose of the occasion changed from a social function to a 'Get-Meredith-to-pay' event. We were well aware that he had promotion in mind and therefore regarded inspectors as God-like figures who might help him on his way to the top; Meredith liked to grease around those in authority.

We reckoned we could make good use of that character-trait and accordingly spread the news that the Inspector was to attend. We also hinted that previous events had shown that promotion came to one of the officers who attended, sometimes within six months. That was enough for Meredith; he put his name down on the sheet.

By this time, Sergeant Bairstow was enjoying the situation and had entered the 'get-Meredith' field. Having achieved a suitable number of attendees, he rang the Boswell Arms at Brantsford and booked us in for a Friday night; then Bairstow stuck out his neck and told the landlord his name was Meredith Dryden and that he would be meeting the entire bill.

Word of this got around to everyone except Sergeant Blaketon, who lacked humour; we didn't inform the Inspector either, in case he objected to the subterfuge. To further our aims, we contrived a situation so that when all twenty-four of us were seated, Meredith was seated next to the Inspector's wife. We knew that would please him and that in such a position, he would be malleable.

Our plans made, we waited for the great night. True to form, Meredith scrounged a lift from a colleague at Brantsford and arrived to find a seating plan at the table. We enjoyed our preliminary drinks, during which Meredith's were paid for by someone who wished to ensure that he remained completely oblivious of our plans, and eventually we were asked to take our places at the table.

As it was a prearranged menu, there were no choices to be made, although the waitress did ask one of us which was Mr Dryden, whereupon she asked Meredith to choose the wines. He did this with pride, revealing a surprisingly good knowledge which impressed the Inspector. The meal was excellent, the companionship good and the night a huge success. After the meal, we sat around the table completely sated and very content with our liqueurs and coffee. Finally, the landlady came to Sergeant Bairstow with the bill for twenty-four dinners and wine.

It was a discreet move, one which passed almost unobserved by the majority of the diners, but Charlie Bairstow pointed towards Meredith and said, "That is Mr Dryden, he's paying."

As she walked towards him bearing the bill on a silver tray, it dawned upon the assembled guests that a historic moment was nigh. The purpose of the night was about to be achieved. We observed the steady progression of the landlady's approach to Meredith's chair. He was engrossed in an animated conversation with the Inspector's wife and failed to notice the impending arrival of the bill.

As the landlady halted at his shoulder, we all watched, hearts beating with anticipation at the arrival of the supreme moment. Meredith Dryden was about to pay for something, for none of us would settle this bill.

"The bill, Mr Dryden," she eased the tray before him. His face said everything. His brain, so finely attuned to the avoidance of paying, especially for anything which was for the consumption of others, must have told him that this was a set-up. He must have instantly realised that everyone — well, almost everyone — at that table, knew what was happening.

Meredith was fully aware that no one would come to his aid; he was on his own in this crisis. He had been well and truly cornered. Sergeant Blaketon was at the far end of the room beyond his reach, and the only person of substance close at hand was the Inspector. I'm sure Meredith realised that the Inspector knew nothing of this plot and so the Inspector was like an innocent babe as he faced the formidable financial skills of Meredith Dryden.

"Sir," we heard Meredith say in a hoarse whisper, "I've forgotten my cheque book — might I ask if you could pay the bill, and I will settle with you tomorrow when I come to the office?"

The Inspector, a leader of men and a man of substance who suddenly found himself being observed by almost every member of Ashfordly and Brantsford Sections, flushed a deep red, but he pulled out his wallet. It was he who had been skilfully cornered, and so he wrote out a cheque for the full amount. To give the fellow credit, he even gave a £1 tip to the staff.

None of us knew what to make of this, except that it was abundantly clear that Meredith had scored yet again.

"We'll have to make it up to the Inspector," I heard Charlie Bairstow say later to Alwyn Foxton. "We all know what it's about, so we'll have to have a whip-round. We'll have to pay our share. The bugger's beaten us again . . ."

"Meredith won't pay," said Alwyn. "The Inspector will finish up paying his share anyway!"

And so it was. We all paid our due amounts into a kitty which was passed over to the Inspector, but we knew that Meredith never paid his share. The Inspector had paid for Meredith's meal — Meredith the Miser had won yet again and had enjoyed another free meal.

But his success was short-lived. Less than three weeks later, he was transferred to a distant station.

CHAPTER 7

With secret course, which no loud storms annoy
Glides the smooth current of domestic joy.
SAMUEL JOHNSON, 1709—84

For a large number of British workers, whether male or
female, there is a clear distinction between their work
and their domestic life. The home, with all its comforts
and traumas, is left firmly behind when a living has to be
earned and throughout the working day, the pressures of
the office or the working environment supersede all but the
most severe of domestic worries or the blissful contentment
of home. It is right that the domestic life of an employee
should rarely intrude into his or her business or work, and
so all but the closest of workmates have no concept of a
colleague's home life and circumstances.

But there are those who work either at home or from
home; rural doctors and vicars are popular examples, as are
the local postmasters or mistresses, shopkeepers, farmers,
sales representatives and many village businessfolk. To that
incomplete list can be added the village policeman.

For many rural bobbies, the village police house is both
home and office. And so it was with me. It was inevitable

that there were times when aspects of my domestic life became inextricably intertwined, albeit in the most pleasant of ways, with my professional duties. Apart from being the police office of Aidensfield, my house was also home to my wife and four tiny children, along with all our hobbies and domestic activities. Like all policemen in that situation, I did endeavour to keep work and leisure completely separate, but at times this was impossible.

There is no doubt that the police house at Aidensfield ranks among the most beautifully located in Yorkshire, and possibly in England. Built in the 1960s on a superb elevated site, it is stoutly constructed of local yellow stone with a red pantile roof. It boasts a lounge with panoramic views, a dining-room and tiny kitchen, with three bedrooms and a bathroom. The garage adjoins and there is a through-passage which separates the house from the garage; off that passage there is an outside toilet and a wash-room. These outbuildings, small as they are, did help to accommodate that awesome range of bulky objects that young families accumulate, such as tricycles, prams and pushchairs. At the other end of the house, the west end, is the office. This is a spacious room with a solid wooden counter and separate entrance. In my time, it was furnished with an official desk, chair and telephone.

The hilltop site, which isolated us from the village below, was enhanced by a steep, mature and well-stocked garden. To the back and front of the house were panoramic views across the North York Moors, the Wolds and the valleys below. In the summer, it was a delight; in the winter, it could be a nightmare because, at times, the winds were so powerful that the garage doors could not be opened, while the carpets and rugs rippled like snakes as powerful draughts invaded our home and rattled the windows. At times, we were very prone to being snowed in; a fact which created frequent notes of disbelief among senior officers who sat in warm offices in distant, low-lying towns.

I must admit there were times when I was sure they thought I was inventing the snow to avoid a winter patrol on my motorcycle. On one occasion, it took me four hours to dig my way out of the garage, after which I was subjected to a telling-off for being late on patrol . . .

But, winter apart, it was a lovely place in which to live and to rear a family. By comparison with many other police houses, it was, and still is, a gem. At that time, of course, the privilege of having an officially provided house was of immense value, especially on a constable's meagre salary with a growing family to support.

Perhaps, at this point, it would be of interest to learn how a young constable qualified for his very first police house. The Aidensfield house was not my first, but in order to progress through a range of police houses, one had to qualify for the first: once into the system, it was a simple matter of being transferred from one to another. The first hurdle was the most difficult.

In my own case, we had married some five years before we were posted to Aidensfield and we began our wedded bliss in a flat at Strensford. We rented this accommodation independently of the police but after three months in that second-floor flat I was summoned to the Superintendent's office.

"Rhea," he said with a glow of benevolence on his face, "a police house has become vacant in the town; it's an end-terrace house with three bedrooms and is not therefore, one of our standard houses. It's a modern house, by the way. But as our most recently married member, you might qualify to occupy it. Now, are you in a position to furnish a house?"

Quick as a flash, in spite of our solitary bed, our dining-table, two fireside chairs and clip rug, I said, "Yes, sir."

He wasn't to know that my scant furnishings would barely fill the kitchen, let alone a complete house, but I did not want this opportunity to evaporate. A modern three-bedroomed house, rent free, was a godsend.

"And do you intend remaining in the Force as a career?" was his next question.

"Yes, sir," I said with as much conviction as I could muster.

"And what about a family, Rhea? You have none, have you?"

"No, sir, not yet."

"And your wife is working is she?"

"For the moment, sir, yes. She's a secretary at the council offices."

He chatted about my future, and about the responsibilities of occupying a police house, and then he said it was mine. I could have the keys next week.

When I told Mary, she was delighted, for our new home was a modern, brick-built house with up-to-date kitchen fittings and beautiful decor. It had a small, pleasant garden and it overlooked the harbour at Strensford with magnificent views of the abbey and old town. It ought to be said, however, that the railway station and some sidings did lie between us and that water. But that was a minor blemish.

When the tide was high, the views across the wide, upper reaches of Strensford harbour were delightful, but when the water was low, it revealed a narrow channel among acres of shining black mud littered with junk which had been deposited over many years. But the house was lovely.

The fact that it was not a standard police house did not worry us. Standard houses were constructed so that when a police family moved from one to another (as they did with staggering frequency), their furnishings and carpets would fit. As a theory, it was fine, but some standard lounges were three inches shorter than others; some bedrooms were narrower or longer than others, and there were many minor variations which made nonsense of the system. Even in standard houses it was difficult to make the furniture fit, and another problem was that the decor which pleased some families was horrific and bizarre in the eyes of others. But it was nice to know that the authorities had our interests at heart.

Our house had been rented by the local police because of a shortage of standard houses in Strensford, but luxuries like fitted carpets or full bedroom suites did not concern us. We hadn't any. Happily, the decorations and exterior paintwork were in good repair.

At that early stage of marriage, we would have had difficulty filling a caravan with our belongings, let alone a semi-detached mansion. Happy with our new home, we settled in and were very content. A few weeks later the Superintendent met me during a patrol.

"Rhea," he said, "I intend carrying out my house inspections and will be starting next week. I shall be calling on you. What is a convenient time?"

I performed some rapid mental gymnastics because I wanted him to come when the tide was full. I knew the harbour view would impress him, so I said, "Next Wednesday, Sir? Would 3 p.m. be suitable?"

He checked his diary and agreed.

When I told Mary, she grew flustered. I had to explain that his visit was not to check upon our cleanliness or her housekeeping ability, but to ascertain whether any repairs or other work were required on the house, either externally or internally.

"If he looks in all the rooms, there's nothing . . . we've two empty bedrooms, nothing in the dining-room . . ." She began to worry about our lack of furniture, and whether we would be asked to vacate it.

I must admit that this did bother me too, particularly as I'd recently assured him I could furnish a home. To cut a long story short, we borrowed from friends a dining suite, a three-piece suite, two single beds, two wardrobes, rugs, carpets and some sundry furnishings. The result was that on the day of the house inspection, our little home looked almost luxurious. All the young constables did this; we regularly borrowed each other's stuff on such occasions.

Because Mary was at work at the appointed hour I stayed to show him around. When the Superintendent arrived, I took him into the lounge, now fully furnished and smelling heavily of polish. A vase of flowers occupied the window ledge and pictures hung from the walls, but he was only interested in the lovely view. It was a fine sunny day and the full harbour glistened in the brilliant light. He rhapsodized over the scene which spread before him and chatted about the yachts and small boats on the water as he admired our superb maritime view.

Then he asked if any maintenance work was required and I said, "No, sir, it's in good repair, inside and out."

"Good, well, as you know, Rhea, we decorate internally every three years and externally every seven. That will be done automatically. If you need urgent work done, such as plumbing leaks, washers on taps and so on, submit Form 29."

"Yes, sir."

"Well, you keep a nice home, Rhea. Give my congratulations to your wife. It's nice to see things looking so well — and you've a nice taste in three-piece suites. PC Radcliffe has that design on his suite too, you know."

Then he smiled and left. The Superintendent was very astute, I decided, and Mary was pleased that he did not venture any further than the lounge. Our impressive view had kept him in one room.

And so we started as occupants of several police houses. We bought more furniture when funds permitted and produced a brood of infants within surprisingly few years. By the time we arrived at Aidensfield, we had, of necessity, to furnish all the rooms to accommodate the six members of our family.

Once again, we were fortunate to be provided with a lovely house and a lounge with a view, even if it did mean regular house inspections. In addition, we had local government bureaucracy to contend with when maintenance or improvements were necessary. This led to several battles. My first concerned the outer passage and washing-room. The passage had a door at each end, and just off it was the room which housed the clothes washing facilities and which also acted as a storeroom. It sounds most convenient, but neither the passage nor the washing-room had windows or lights. In the passageway, an open door would provide light during the daytime, but the wash-room could have served better as a photographer's dark-room.

So I made application, on Form 29, for a light to be fitted in the windowless washing-room. Then we would be able to use it for that purpose. The Superintendent rejected my request on the grounds that it was an 'improvement'; improvements to police authority houses needed special approval from up high, from bodies like the Standing Joint Committee and the County Architect. To reach them, my application would have to proceed via Headquarters' departments and the Chief Constable himself! For reasons he did not explain, the Superintendent refused to forward my report to them; our local 'official channels' terminated upon his desk. There seemed no way to by-pass that blockage.

I did try by explaining that it was impossible to work in that room and that, in its present form, it was useless for its intended purpose, or indeed any other. He continued to utter 'improvement' as his excuse for refusing to allow my report to reach other decision makers. I grew more determined and renewed my campaign by tackling it from another angle.

My next Form 29 suggested that an outside light was necessary to eliminate possible danger to callers at the police house. I suggested that its best position would be above the passage's north-facing door. It would then shine along the passage at night (if the door was open) and would also shine along the entire frontage of the house. I thought it might even shine into the washing-room if two doors were left open!

That was rejected too, again by the Superintendent. Now even more determined. I re-applied for a light to be fitted outside the office door. This time, my Form 29 pointed out the possible danger to the public who might stumble over the steps and who might then sue the Standing Joint Committee for damages or compensation . . .

This time, I got an external light fitted — but it was over the door of the police office and its welcome light did not shine into the passage or the wash-room. When eventually I left the police house at Aidensfield, that washing-room and passage were still without a light. We had to squeeze our washing-machine into the tiny kitchen, no mean feat when it daily washed mountains of nappies.

Also under the heading of 'improvement' was my suggestion that some radiators be run off the little domestic coke boiler.

This tiny furnace was installed in the kitchen and its fierce heat filled the room and heated the water; even in summer, we had to keep it stoked up to cope with masses of baths, nappies and kiddy clothes. We lost gallons of perspiration and I reckoned it would keep two or three central heating radiators well supplied. But because this was an 'improvement', it was not permitted. My Form 29 was rejected.

Then the pipes of this boiler began to make frightening noises. Narrow pipes connected the boiler to the mains water supply and to the hot water tank upstairs, and they began to rattle and vibrate as the heat intensified. In time, I grew very alarmed and rang the Superintendent's office about it. He returned my call to say that such noises were normal in the plumbing world. He expressed this opinion without hearing the racket they made. I felt the noise was far from normal but realised that once again, I was battling against bureaucracy. I waited for a while and the noise grew worse; a friend said the pipes sounded as if they were blocked, a common occurrence in hot water pipes hereabouts because the lime deposits from the local water furred them.

Repeated requests via Form 29 met with nil response and this frustrated me. Being country born and bred, I was used to coping with my own domestic maintenance — we would never call in anyone to do jobs we could do ourselves such as painting, decorating, running repairs to machinery, tiling, pointing — in fact, anything and everything. But as occupants of a police house, we were instructed not to attempt any repairs or work, not even the replacement of a tap washer. I found these restrictions very frustrating.

The clattering grew worse. We reached the stage where we were frightened to light the fire because of the clamour coming from those pipes and this meant we had no hot water. Then came salvation. It came in the shape of a memo from the Superintendent which announced he was coming to conduct a house inspection.

I recognised the opportunity presented by his visit.

He was due at 11.30 a.m. one Friday, a busy day for nappies and infant washing, and so I arranged for the boiler to be well stoked-up and the flues opened wide to coincide with his visit. I was confident that the resultant noise from those pipes would terrify him. It didn't matter which part of the house he was visiting at the time, because I was sure the din could be heard throughout a building of castle proportions.

He came, inspected, had a coffee and asked about the pipes. After all, a succession of Forms 29 had made him aware of the problem. I said they were worse, upon which he ventured into the kitchen. It was now uncomfortably hot as the coke performed its heating role and he looked at the offending pipes. There was nothing to see — they were just two pipes running up the wall.

And then, almost as if they knew he was standing there, they performed on cue. It was just as if a giant with a big hammer was inside, banging and hammering to be let out and the whole house vibrated as the pipes visibly shuddered in their moment of triumph.

"My God!" he panted, rushing from the kitchen, white-faced and anxious . . .

Early next day, a plumber arrived. After an examination, he said the pipes were almost blocked; the hot water was trying to rise through the cold pipe and had we not called him, there could have been a shocking explosion . . .

My final Form 29 confirmed that the pipes were working normally.

In such minor ways, my work and domestic life overlapped, although there were other instances. For example, at 4 a.m. one morning, a lorry driver knocked me out of bed and roused the entire family, simply to ask directions to Home Farm. On another occasion, at 6.30 a.m. one day when I was on holiday, a farmer came to the door to seek a pig licence. When I said I was on holiday and that he should go to Ashfordly Police Station, he said, "Well, you're t' bobby, aren't you?"

I issued his licence.

In many ways, it was my young family which further involved me in this curious mixture of duty and home. One day, when I was enjoying time off during the week, I decided to do some gardening. I claim no green-fingered skills but felt that if I dug enough holes and cut enough grass, I could believe I had achieved something positive. During this enterprise, Mary asked if I would look after the children while she went to Ashfordly to do some shopping. I agreed, so she jumped into our car and cheerfully vanished towards the market town.

The day was fine and warm, and I was thoroughly enjoying myself. The children were playing in the garden behind the house and I had fixed up a plastic bath half full of water which they were using as a paddling pool. After about an hour, I broke from my chores to make myself and the children a cool drink.

"Where's Charles?" I asked.

"Gone to the toilet," said Elizabeth.

He was only three and I accepted her answer. I put his drink on the step and settled down to await his return. He did not come. I went indoors and looked at both toilets; he wasn't there. I went into his room and looked in the bed, the wardrobe and under the bed. He wasn't there either.

Knowing that children love to play hide and seek, I searched the whole house as only a policeman can but found no sign of him. Now more than a little worried, I checked my office, the garage, the passage and the washing-room with its darkness. There was no Charles. I re-checked all the beds by pulling back the covers and looking underneath, then I searched the pram and finally tackled the garden. There were shrubs, trees and plants, a cold frame and plenty of long grass to conceal a little boy, but my frantic hunt failed to locate him.

By now, my concern was becoming genuine alarm and I made several more sorties into the house, the garage and the garden. And then I wondered if he'd jumped into the car to accompany Mary?

That seemed the only logical explanation, but the more I thought about it, the more I realised he hadn't. She'd have mentioned it, surely? She'd wanted a moment or two to herself . . . I'd seen her leave alone . . .

I stood in the middle of my garden, by this time a very worried man. Where on earth could he have gone? Even though the garden gates were shut, I went onto the main road and looked up and down. I was able to gaze along almost half a mile of highway, but there was no sign of the toddler. He'd vanished into thin air and I was in a dreadful dilemma. I could not leave the rest of them alone while I went to seek Charles, and I began to understand the problems of some parents. What could I do? Anyone else would have telephoned the police!

With this possibility rapidly gaining strength in my mind, I realised I couldn't remember what he was wearing. Of course, a three-year-old lad wandering about unaccompanied wouldn't be too difficult to locate . . .

I decided upon yet another thorough search of the premises. It drew a blank. Outside, the other children played happily, quite oblivious to my growing alarm, and at last I went into my office and dialled the Ashfordly Police Station number. It rang and rang; there was no reply. They're never there when they're wanted, I grumbled! I decided to ring the Divisional Police Station at Malton to ask if a car was patrolling in the Aidensfield area. That was quite possible because I was not on duty, and the area would not be left totally without a patrol. If there was a car nearby, it would be radio-equipped and the driver would keep his eyes open for any missing child.

I began to formulate my request; I would ask the driver to keep observations for a child aged three, with light brown hair, clothing unknown, who might be wandering . . .

As the phone began to ring, someone knocked on my office door. What a time to call! I was off duty anyway! Slamming down the phone, I opened the door. A lorry driver was standing there and he was holding Charles in his arms. His vehicle was parked outside.

"Found this kid," he thrust the infant towards me. "Wandering down t' hill . . . biggest wonder he didn't get killed . . . some parents . . . thought you'd know who belonged him . . ."

"Er, yes," I didn't know how to respond. "Er, come in . . . have a cup of tea . . ."

"No, got a schedule to keep. You know him then?"

"Yes," I said, humbly.

"Good, thought you would. Give his mum a rocket, eh? For letting him get out like that . . . stupid bloody parents . . ."

And off he went.

I hugged Charles with relief, being unable to explain to the little fellow the problems he had created. I decided that my immediate priority was to fix child-proof locks on the garden gate, but also decided not to tell a soul about this. Not even Mary.

My latter plans went haywire too. A lady in the village had been present when the lorry driver collected the wandering child and had directed him to the police house. She told Mary . . .

The whole village knew too. I was suitably humbled, embarrassed and chastened. And little Charles never batted an eyelid, although I did fix child-proof locks to the gates. Ever since, I've had sympathy for parents whose children go wandering.

Another personal domestic crisis concerned Margaret, our two-year-old daughter. From the moment she could crawl, she could climb. She climbed the stairs and chairs, steps and trees, bookshelves and pantry shelves. She could climb onto the car bonnet, onto the motorcycle and onto the backs of settees and indeed upon almost any piece of domestic equipment or furniture. At times, I felt she had a wonderful future as a rock-climber or steeplejack and this was confirmed when she managed to climb out of her bedroom window on to the outer ledge.

She remained there as I pleaded with her not to move; with her safely indoors, I then secured the window, but soon she was climbing up the shelves of the wardrobe and sitting on top. On one occasion, she was marooned up an apple tree and on another managed to climb into a fireside chair and from there gain access to the mantelpiece. From these escapades, she was unscathed.

But, inevitably, an accident was bound to happen; one day she would fall and hurt herself.

One lunchtime, I returned from a motorcycle patrol to find Mary holding little Margaret over the kitchen sink as blood poured from her tiny mouth. The accident had happened only seconds earlier. Without even removing my crash helmet, I took one look at the injury and found a gaping wound inside her mouth.

Without asking for an explanation, I rang the village doctor who, fortunately, was at home having his lunch. "Bring her down," he said. I packed some cotton wool over the wound to stem the flow and rushed Margaret to the doctor. Mary couldn't come — she had the other children to look after.

"No good," the doctor said instantly. "She needs hospital treatment, stitches. You take her there now, I'll ring to say you're on the way."

With the tiny child sitting in the front seat of my car and holding her cheek against the wad of cotton wool, I furiously drove the seventeen miles into Malton to the hospital where a doctor met me. In moments, my little daughter was lying on an operating table, without anaesthetic, as the doctor examined the wound and prepared to stitch it.

"What happened to her?" he asked.

"I don't know," I had to admit. "I didn't ask . . ."

"It'll mend," he said, producing a huge curved needle. I winced; I began to feel emotional at the thought of that tiny child suffering as I submitted her to this instant surgery. Margaret, God bless her, never cried and never complained. It was awful, watching her tiny frame being subjected to this treatment.

During this work, a nurse hovered around the theatre and as the doctor began to skilfully sew the wound, she came over to me.

"Some parents!" she said. "Look at that poor child . . . and you'd think they'd bring her themselves . . . the police get all the rotten jobs to do . . . Fancy you having to do this . . ."

As she ranted, it became clear that she had no idea that this was *my* child; the fact that I was sitting there in full police motorcycling uniform had obviously led her into thinking I was doing my duty by protecting some neglected youngster . . .

She continued her verbal onslaught against callous and thoughtless parents as the doctor continued his work on the mouth wound. Then she produced a sheet of paper.

"Child's name?" she asked.

"Margaret Rhea, aged two," I said.

"Father's name?"

"Nicholas Rhea," I watched her write down these details. "Address?"

"The Police House Aidensfield," I said.

"No," she threw me one of those withering glances that one expects from matrons, not nurses, "the child's address, not yours!"

"That is the child's address," I said. "She's my child."

"Oh," she said. "I had no idea . . . I thought . . ."

"She'll be fine now," the doctor had finished. "I've put three stitches in, they'll wither away in time and there'll be no mark. It's young, clean flesh, so it will quickly mend. There's no other injury."

"Thanks, Doctor," and I carried little Margaret out to my waiting car and drove home. Other than a puffy cheek, she seemed no worse and never once complained. When she arrived home, she sat in her high-chair and ate her dinner.

She behaved as if nothing had happened and the wound did not appear to give her pain.

I ate my lunch too, still upset by the trauma of seeing the doctor working so expertly and coolly upon her. "Mary," I asked, "what happened to her?"

"She was climbing up the shelves of the bookcase," Mary told me. "I went into the lounge just as she got to the top — she fell off and her face hit the edge of the coal scuttle . . ."

Mary began to weep so I comforted her as, quite unabashed, Margaret continued with her meal.

In spite of our efforts to prevent her, she continued to climb for some years afterwards, but never with such dramatic effect.

Perhaps the funniest incident which involved both my work and my private life occurred one February morning. This is the sequence of events — my involvement came sometime after the beginning of the saga, but it is best to relate it from the start.

Around one o'clock on the morning in question, my mother and father were dragged from their bed by a telephone call from the CID at York. It came at a time when there was concern about letter bombs and the detective was calling from the GPO Sorting Office.

"Is that Mrs Rhea?" the detective asked my mother. He then provided the correct address to make sure he was speaking to the right person.

"Yes," answered my mother, bleary-eyed and sleepy.

"This is York CID," said the voice. "I'm ringing from the GPO Sorting Office at York. This is a difficult enquiry, Mrs Rhea, and I don't want to alarm you, but are you expecting a parcel from anyone?"

"Well," said my mother, not yet appreciating the problem, "I might be, it's my birthday tomorrow . . . er today . . ."

"Ah!" There was some relief at this response. "And you have no enemies? You, or your husband are not in sensitive work, are you? It's not the sort of work that would attract, well, a letter bomb?"

"No . . . well, I don't think so . . ."

"Well, the point is, there's a suspicious package here and it's addressed to you."

The detective took immense pains to describe his problem without being too alarmist, but it seemed that as the GPO sorters were dealing with the night's influx of mail, one of them discovered a parcel which began to emit ticking sounds. As everyone dived for cover, the parcel was placed in a sand-filled bin designed to cope with exploding parcels. As it sat there, the entire staff of the sorting office took cover and waited for the bang. As they settled down behind whatever protection they could find, the police were called. And so the official procedures were set in motion.

The busy task of sorting the mail came to a halt and the district's mail was thus delayed until the CID arrived and the offending parcel was dealt with, probably by Bomb Disposal experts. One of the detectives, whom I shall call Gordon, arrived and looked at the offending object in the bin. It had now stopped ticking. Heads peeped above the counters and around walls as Gordon bravely scrutinised the parcel. Then he picked it up.

It promptly started ticking. Everyone dived for cover.

He threw it back into the bin and vanished below a sturdy counter. Everyone waited for it to explode, but it did not. And so it lay at peace in its protective bin as the entire staff and the police hid behind their benches. They waited for a long, long time, but nothing happened. There was no bang and it had stopped ticking.

Gordon approached it again. The address on the parcel was legible; it bore my mother's name, hence the morning call to her.

"I've no idea what it might be," she said. "If it is a birthday present, it might have been sent by my daughter and son-in-law in London."

"What do they do?" asked the detective.

"He's in the Metropolitan Police in London . . ."

"Then there could be risks . . . someone might be hitting back at him . . ."

Having elicited this information, Gordon rang Scotland Yard to check against the possibility of attacks against the police, and then rang my brother-in-law at his London home to explain the problem. But neither he nor my sister had sent the parcel. They were then asked if they knew anyone else who might have sent it; they suggested it could have come from my brother who lives in the Shetlands. He works for BP, and so there could have been some sinister links with a letter bomb.

As a consequence, he and his family were roused about 1.30 a.m. and the questions were repeated; they had not sent a parcel. Further checks were made with the security services, but there was no known campaign against our institutions.

My brother, however, was asked if *he* knew who might have sent a parcel, if indeed it was a genuine parcel, then he said, "My brother at Aidensfield might have sent it. He's a policeman too."

With the intrigue growing stronger, the mystery growing deeper and the mail growing further delayed, Gordon now rang me. By this time, it was around two o'clock on a chill February morning. I staggered into my cold office to take his call. At that stage, I knew nothing of the drama.

"Nick," he said. "It's Gordon at York."

We had been at training-school together and knew one another fairly well.

"York?" I muttered through a haze of sleepiness. "What's happened? It's two o'clock in the morning."

"We have a parcel addressed to your mother," and he patiently related the story so far. "Now, I had no idea the lady was *your* mother — I've been ringing Scotland Yard, the Shetlands, the Special Branch, GPO Security, MI5 . . ."

"Oh?" this sounded important.

"So, Nick," he asked, with a hint of exhaustion, "yesterday, did you post a parcel to your mother?"

"No," I said. "I sent her a card with a gift token inside. I didn't send a parcel . . . it's her birthday today, so I suppose someone . . ."

"Oh, bloody hell . . ." There was a long silence at the other end of the telephone, then he said, "Hang on, I'll have another look at it. We can't decipher the postmark you see, and we're worried about touching it . . . I'm sure it's your mother's name on it . . ."

But he did touch it. It was sitting in its secure bin, and he lifted it to check the postmark. It started to tick again. He dropped it back inside the bin and dived for cover as I waited on the line.

Everyone was still under cover, but eventually he returned to the telephone, breathless.

"God, this is awful," he said. "The bloody thing could go off at any minute . . . I'm safe behind a screen here . . ."

"You're a brave bloke to tackle it like you have," I said.

"I'm not," he said. "I'm stupid. I've been to a night club for a few pints and don't know what I'm doing really."

As this conversation continued, Mary appeared at my side. "What's the matter?" she asked. "Are you talking about your mother. Has something happened? Is she ill?"

"No," I said, "it's the CID. They think someone's sent her a bomb . . ."

Mary began to chuckle. "A parcel? Brown paper, with white string? A sticky label on the front? The address written in black ballpoint ink?"

As she described her parcel, I relayed the words to Gordon.

"This is the one," he growled. "Bloody hell! What a night! The description fits. Did your wife send it, Nick? Has she sent a bomb to her mother-in-law or something?"

"Did you send it?" I asked Mary, my feet like ice-blocks on the cold office floor.

"Yes, why, what's wrong?"

I explained about the chaos in York and the terror she had inflicted upon the Post Office, the police and probably

GPO Security. The whole of the region's mail would be delayed and several sorters were close to having heart attacks.

"It's a pair of scissors," she said. "A pair of electric scissors, for cutting material to make dresses."

My heart sank.

"Is there a battery in?"

"Yes, I fitted it before we posted it . . ."

And so, when pressure was applied to that parcel in certain places, the scissors began to snip within their box . . .

I apologised profusely to everyone and rang my mother to wish her a happy birthday.

CHAPTER 8

The death of a dear friend would go near to
make a man look sad.
WILLIAM SHAKESPEARE, 1564—1616

Every Autumn the children of Aidensfield waited for the donkeys to return to Lingfield Farm. These were seaside donkeys. During the summer, they spent their time on the beach at Strensford where, day after day, they patiently carried laughing children backwards and forwards along the sands. Adorned in brightly-coloured bridles bearing their names, with ribboned top-knots on their heads and neat little saddles on their backs, they had been a part of the Strensford beach scene since Victorian times.

They worked very hard but were always models of tolerance and patience. Perhaps their gentleness was due to the fact that they were not overworked; during their working week, for example, they were subjected to conditions about their rest periods. They enjoyed one day off in every three, with three meals a day and an hour for lunch. Their working day did not exceed eight hours and they were inspected regularly by a veterinary surgeon. In some respects, their working conditions were better than those of police officers!

During the winter, they came inland for their holidays where they were boarded out at selected farms. Jack Sedgewick at Lingfield Farm, Aidensfield, had for years taken five of the donkeys from Strensford. As a rule, they arrived by cattle truck at the end of the summer season and remained until the Whitsuntide bank holiday. They occupied a rough, hummocky paddock where they seemed to thrive on the wealth of thistles and other vegetation which had little appeal to other beasts.

They had a range of small outbuildings, some without doors, which served as stables. These contained plenty of hay as bedding and for food, and there was an outdoor water-trough adequately fed with spring water. Some shrub-like hawthorn trees added variety to the paddock's undulating landscape and provided slender shelter against the winter storms.

Jack Sedgewick, a large and kindly man, knew that his guests required regular exercise otherwise they would grow fat and lazy. This presented no problem because he encouraged local children to come along and play with his little group of donkeys. He taught the youngsters how to care for them; to make sure their feet were trimmed regularly; to coax them to their halters and to feed them with the right kind of things. Some children rode them, and a little girl even persuaded one donkey, called Lucy, to jump over a small artificial fence.

It was very clear that the donkeys loved the children and the children loved the donkeys; indeed, there is some kind of mysterious affinity between small children and donkeys. These gentle and calm animals, with their big, soft eyes and cuddly long ears — called 'errant wings' by G. K. Chesterton — are so lovable. It wasn't all smooth and jolly, however. The occasional bout of stubbornness from a donkey who, for reasons best known to itself did not want to play, sometimes upset the youngsters, while a sudden session of braying made them jump with fright before dissolving into laughter. For the children, these minor upsets were lessons in themselves.

For one thing, they taught the children they could not have everything all their own way, even with donkeys.

One winter, Lingfield Farm accepted its usual complement of five donkeys. They were Lucy, Linda, Betty, Bonny and Fred, and it was Fred who thought he was a human being. He loved to enter the house whenever possible; he loved to nose his way into small crowds and it was not unknown for him to poke his head through the open dining-room window of the farm whenever the family was having a meal. Calm, lovable and cuddly with his thick, grey coat and distinctive black cross on his back, he was a pet and a favourite.

Always popular with the children, he allowed them to ride him through the fields and lanes and when he got some distance from the farm, he would occasionally issue a blood-curdling braying noise, his way of checking whether any other donkey, male or female, was living nearby. The children used him in a Nativity Play at school where he stood as still as a rock and solemnly overlooked the model crib they had made. His acting was superb. From time to time, I saw Fred plodding along the lanes with his tiny charges making a fuss of him and I was pleased he provided the bairns with such pleasurable activity. These children would grow up to appreciate animals and their needs, and it was all due to their pal, Fred.

Then Fred disappeared.

It wasn't difficult to imagine the anguish and concern among the children and their parents. Indeed, poor old Jack Sedgewick was most upset too. He rang me just before ten o'clock one morning in April.

"Mr Rhea," he said, with his voice showing traces of emotion. "Ah've lost yan o' them donkeys. Fred, it is. Sometime since last night. Do you reckon 'e could 'ave been stolen?"

"I'll come down to the farm," I assured him. To my knowledge, there had not been an outbreak of donkey thefts or moke-nappings and I couldn't imagine who would do such a thing. My own immediate view was that Fred had probably got through an insecure gate and wandered off. I felt he would turn up in due course.

When I arrived at Lingfield Farm, I found Jack Sedgewick and a small knot of children standing at the gate of the paddock which contained the other donkeys. The animals were standing together in a corner, watching us; if only they could talk, I thought. I halted my motorbike and parked it against a wall.

"Good of you to come down so quick, Mr Rhea," he said. "Fred's gone . . . He was there last night . . . I fed him, Mr Rhea . . . I took his bridle off . . ."

The children were all talking at once so I held up my hands to indicate silence.

"Just a minute!" I laughed. "I can't hear anybody if you all talk at once. So, Jack. You first."

"I found him gone," one little girl couldn't contain her worry.

"Aye," Jack confirmed. "Young Denise here came down to t' field about half-eightish. She came to feed 'em all, and noticed Fred wasn't there."

"Was the gate open or shut, Denise?" I asked her. She would be about eleven years old.

"Shut, Mr Rhea. It swings shut by itself."

I tried it. It was fastened with a hunting sneck, a type of fastening which comprised a length of wood suspended from two chains. It had a carved notch and it slotted into a bracket on the gatepost. It was easy to open when on horseback; this was done by easing it back with a riding crop, hence its name. I eased back the sneck and let the gate stand wide open, but it swung slowly shut by its own weight and the sneck slid home. The gate was then secure. For this reason, it seemed unlikely that the gate could be accidentally left open. But I knew it was not impossible. If it had been opened only sufficiently wide for a child to emerge, it might not have had the impetus or weight to latch itself properly after only a small movement.

"Who saw him last?" was my next question.

"We did," came a chorus of voices.

"Where?"

"In the village, last night," they told me. I asked one girl, the tallest of the group, to explain. She said half a dozen of them had taken Fred into the village for a walk and a ride.

"Did anything happen, or did anyone say anything about him? Or to him? Can you remember?" I put to her.

"We all took turns riding," she said seriously. "He wasn't upset or anything."

"Did anybody say anything to him? To you, maybe? About Fred? Was anyone angry or annoyed with him for anything?"

I was trying to establish whether anyone had threatened to take the animal away either as a joke or as a serious threat. The antics of the children and Fred could have upset someone.

"There was that man in the pub," said one small girl.

"What man was that?" I asked.

"We got crisps and lemonade at the pub."

"The Brewers Arms?"

"Yes. We went to the door like we always do."

"And what about the man? What did he do?"

"He smacked Fred on the nose," said one of them. "Just fun, though, he was just playing."

"Maybe that's upset Fred!" I smiled. "Maybe he's taken the huff and gone off to sulk! So what happened exactly, Denise?"

"We had Fred with us. We wanted some crisps and things, so we went to the pub. Fred followed us in. Or he tried to. He poked his nose over the counter and this man clonked him on the nose, just in fun it was. Fred backed away . . . that was all."

"And after your walk with him, you put him back in the paddock with the others?"

"Yes, we gave him some hay, patted him for a minute or two and then we went home."

"And did you shut that gate?"

They all swore that it was properly closed. Jack Sedgewick said he did his rounds after ten o'clock that night and noticed nothing amiss. I looked at the lanes which led away from the donkey paddock; if it had got out, it could have wandered into the village, or into the surrounding woods and hills, or even along the river bank. It could be anywhere.

"What about your buildings, Jack? Have they been searched?"

The children provided the answer; they had searched everywhere on the farm before calling me.

"I'll report him as missing," I said. "Now, how about organising a hunt for him?"

And so I organised a small hunt around the likely places in and around Aidensfield; there were empty farm buildings, woods, copses, fields and so on. I allocated a safe place for groups of these children to search; each group comprised three for safety reasons.

Jack said he would walk his own land this morning to check ditches and other likely places, and I decided to ask questions around the village. After all, someone might have spotted a lone donkey trotting along the road. I told them I'd keep Mr Sedgewick informed of developments.

A couple of hours later, I was in the Post Office asking about Fred. Several people were there. They were asking for postal orders and stamps, and some were at the grocery counter. As I chatted and spread the news about Fred, a man in hiking gear walked in to buy some fruit and drinks. He noticed me, but he was not a local man. I didn't know him.

"Ah, Officer," he said, his keen grey eyes showing bright in his weathered face. "Just the fellow. I've just come through Plantation Wood," and he showed me his route on a map clipped to his belt. "And there's a dead donkey just off the footpath . . ."

"Dead donkey?" I almost shouted. "Are you sure?"

"Well," he seemed surprised at my reaction. "Well, it was lying down . . . maybe it wasn't dead . . ."

I asked him to pinpoint the exact place and noticed that everyone in the shop was listening. We identified the place as being about half-way along the bridleway between High Nab and Cross Plain, where it ran alongside Plantation Wood.

As I confirmed the details, the shop emptied rapidly and the customers scurried to their homes. They seemed to have been galvanized into action at the news. I decided to walk back to Jack Sedgewick's farm and break the news to him, then I would have to break the news to the children and decide whether or not to take them to the scene. I was sure Jack would help me to deal with the corpse.

"A dead donkey?" he gasped when I located him down his fields.

"So the man said," I replied.

"Right, come wi' me, Mr Rhea, and be sharp," and he led me to his implement shed. He started the engine of one of his tractors and bade me climb aboard. And off we rushed towards Plantation Wood, the tractor bouncing and bumping along the rough farm tracks. There was a definite note of urgency in his actions.

"What's the panic, Jack?" I shouted above the noise of the engine.

"A dead donkey!" he shouted back. "I 'ope it's not poor awd Fred, but nobody's ever seen a dead donkey, Mr Rhea. Did tha know that? It's reckoned ti be good luck to see yan. An' we all need a spot o' good luck."

He accelerated across the fields and from my uncomfortable perch beside his seat, I could now see a straggly line of local people. They were all rushing in the same direction, using a short cut from the village.

"Are they all going to see it?" I shouted at him.

"Aye, likely. Word soon gets about when summat like this 'appens. A dead donkey's a rare thing."

As we drew nearer I could see the distinctive figure of the hiker leading the way. Several children had also joined the march. The news had spread with amazing speed. Jack's tractor pushed its way through the throng of people and we arrived, breathless almost, at the same time as the head of the procession. The hiker, baffled by this turn of events, was standing and pointing.

"It's gone," he said, opening his arms wide in an expression of puzzlement. "It was here, I saw it. And it's gone. It was lying right there!" and he stamped the ground with his boot.

And so the villagers never saw their dead donkey.

This is one of those peculiar legends which is supposed to have been started by Charles Dickens; it is said that no one has ever seen a dead donkey and if the news reached a village that a donkey was dying, everyone went to have a look. The legend has probably arisen from a belief that donkeys will wander off to seek a secret place to die.

We turned the tractor around and chugged back to Lingfield Farm.

"Could yon 'ave been Fred?" asked Jack.

"Who else?" I said. "Mebbe he was just resting."

"Aye," said Jack. "Mebbe. Mebbe he'll come back. Donkeys can live wild, tha knaws. Ah've 'eard of one living twelve years in a wood . . . Fred'll come back."

The children were pleased it wasn't Fred who had died, but the mystery caused all sorts of rumours. People went back several times to see if the donkey reappeared but it never did. And Fred never returned to the farm. His companions showed no sign of distress at his continuing absence and the children did get over their sorrow. Later that spring, Lucy, Linda, Betty and Bonny went back to their beach without Fred, and no one ever saw him again.

To this day, I do not know what happened to him. In my official report, I recorded him as 'Missing' because there was no evidence of theft.

But could that donkey have been Fred lying dead in the wood? Is there a mystery about dead donkeys that has never been revealed? Or did Fred find a new home somewhere?

I do not know. But I have never seen a dead donkey.

Among the lesser known duties of the village policeman are those connected with contagious diseases of animals.

During our training-courses, we were told about anthrax, foot and mouth disease, sheep scab and sheep pox, swine fever, tuberculosis, cattle plague, fowl pest, rabies, atrophic rhinitis, epizootic lymphangitis, pleuro-pneumonia, bovine tuberculosis, sarcoptic parasitic mange, glanders and farcy and other exotic sounding plagues which produced devastating results and misery among farmers.

In the event of an outbreak, or even a suspected outbreak of any of these diseases, it was vital that immediate action was taken by the police, the Ministry of Agriculture, Fisheries and Food and the owner of the livestock. Police action involved the enforcement of a multitude of rules and regulations and the serving of a document called 'Form A'.

As many of our training-school instructors were city types, I'm sure they did not know the effect of, or the reason for, Form A. The result was that we emerged from training-school with the knowledge that if a cow frothed at the mouth or a pig was sick we served Form A. It all seemed very puzzling, and it was not until I worked in a rural area, where domestic livestock is so important to farmers and to the nation's economy, that the real purpose and importance of Form A registered in my mind.

Form A was a printed document which had to be completed by a police officer who suspected an outbreak of one of the diseases I have listed. He completed the form with the name and address of the farm, or even a portion of the farm in question such as a cattle shed or pigsty, and formally delivered a copy to the farmer. For most diseases, copies were also sent to the Ministry of Agriculture, Fisheries and Food at local and national level, the local council, and to various police stations. The effect of this document was to bring to a standstill all movements of animals in and out of the suspect premises until a Ministry vet had carried out his inspection. If he declared the animal(s) to be free from disease, the restrictions were lifted and life returned to normal. If he confirmed the disease, another set of procedures swung into action which could lead to the killing of a solitary pig on a small unit or the slaughter of a complete herd of pedigree cattle on a dairy farm. The precise action depended upon the disease in question; I have outlined the general procedures.

Form A was just one small part of the entire system, but as a whole, the impact of the rules and regulations did appear successful. For example, swine fever had practically been eliminated, sheep-dipping had virtually abolished sheep scab and strict import regulations kept rabies at bay. I never did know of a horse which caught epizootic lymphangitis and the last outbreak of pleuropneumonia was in 1898. We knew, therefore, that a major outbreak of a serious and contagious animal disease was very unlikely, and it's fair to say there were several false alarms, albeit with good intent. No chances were taken. Every suspicion was treated with the utmost care and attention.

In our county (the North Riding of Yorkshire), all police officers were appointed Inspectors under the Diseases of Animals Act; in some counties, only sergeants and those with higher rank carried this responsibility and in some city areas, there might be just one such designated inspector within a police force. In a large rural area, it made sense for all officers to have the powers thus conferred upon him or her and this meant that in addition to normal criminal law and police procedures, we had to be fully conversant with the statutes and procedures relating to this huge and at times complex subject.

In some areas, members of the Ministry of Agriculture's staff carried out these duties and during my time at Aidensfield, there was a growing feeling that all such work should be carried out by civilian inspectors. The authorities felt that this aspect of police work should be gradually phased out. Both the police and the farmers greeted this possible change with mixed feelings. For the police, it gave them a marvellous insight into rural life and helped them perform their wide range of other duties, while the farmers welcomed a uniform presence rather than a plainclothes person wandering about their premises, especially in times of strife.

It was during these slow but relentless changes that the country suffered a huge and devastating outbreak of foot and mouth disease. The awful effects of it filtered down to Reg Lumley's herd at West Gill Farm, Aidensfield.

I learned of the outbreak in October through the newspapers. A report said that foot and mouth disease had been confirmed at Oswestry in Shropshire, and that the police were faced with the task of tracing 2,500 animals which had been sold in the local market shortly before the disease had been discovered. It was a huge task; the cattle could be anywhere in the United Kingdom and every one of them could be carrying the virus. The problem was that the licensing system was not fool proof; bad writing on licences; missing ear-tag numbers which are so vital in the positive identification of a particular beast; and sheer carelessness in record keeping, meant that many cattle would never be traced. They could pass on the disease.

During an epidemic, a contact animal was often identified only when a new outbreak occurred many miles from the point of sale. Meanwhile, it had infected other animals, some of which had been moved away, and so the hunt continued. Foot and mouth disease spreads so rapidly that within five days of that original outbreak, fourteen English counties were declared Controlled Areas. Markets were prohibited and farmers guarded their farm entrances, allowing no one to enter unless their clothing and feet were disinfected.

This huge, fast spreading outbreak was one of the few occasions when members of the general public were inconvenienced. Its awful impact and consequences were such that it pricked the communal conscience of the public as never before. For probably the first time, the great British public knew something of the drama being played out on the farms of their countryside.

At Leeds and Bradford Airport, for example, passengers bound for Ireland had to walk over disinfected mats; the RAC Rally was cancelled; two hundred members of the Second Battalion of the Royal Anglian Regiment were drafted in to fight the outbreak near Shrewsbury; National Hunt racing was called off; the import of fruit, nuts and fresh meat was restricted on the Isle of Man; Christmas trees became scarce due to the restrictions imposed on movements to and from land, and farmers even had to get permission to vote in a by-election. All dogs within five miles of an infected place had to be confined and even poultry movements were restricted.

300 extra veterinary surgeons were drafted in, along with 2,500 ancillary workers; there were fourteen control centres in the country and everyone involved worked fifteen hours per day. All police leave was cancelled and the troops were called in to help with many of the heavy tasks. Burial of the slaughtered animals was one example where military hardware and skills proved most useful.

One paper summed it up like this: "Two brothers came home to find a cow frothing at the mouth. They shut themselves and their families inside the house. Men from the Ministry came to slaughter and bury; the farm was quarantined and red and white 'Keep Out' notices were erected around the boundaries. Policemen arrived and moved into a hut near the farm gate to stop visitors; the local market was cancelled and a pin was stuck in a map at the Foot and Mouth Control Headquarters."

The fear generated by this outbreak can scarcely be imagined; the far-reaching consequences of the disease caused every farmer to barricade himself in his farm and to take every possible precaution to safeguard his own herd. And it was during this atmosphere that I got a call from Reg Lumley.

"Can thoo come, Mr Rhea?" he sounded almost in tears.

"What's up, Reg?" I felt that I needn't have asked.

"Yan o' my coos is frothing," he said.

"Oh my God!"

My heart sank; it looked as if we had foot and mouth in this area, in Aidensfield. I could not comprehend the consequences.

"I'll call the Ministry," I told him. "I won't come down to the farm, I might pick up the disease on my feet. Can you arrange a system of disinfectant at the gate, Reg? A bath or summat will do for folks to walk through. Make folks paddle through it going in and out."

"Aye," he said slowly. "Ah've been preparing, just in case. Ah've got a load of disinfectant and some waterproofs . . . Ah'll see to t' gate; Ah'll chain it up to keep traffic out."

Over the past weeks, as the disease had spread across the nation, I had been issued with some red and white 'Keep Out' posters and so, for the first time during my duties at Aidensfield, I found myself typing out Form A. It had Reg Lumley's name and address on it, and where it asked for the name of the suspected premises, I typed 'The whole of the premises of West Gill Farm, Aidensfield.'

As force procedure demanded, I compiled a telegram for transmission to the Ministry of Agriculture, Fisheries and Food (Animal Health Division) at Tolworth, Surbiton, Surrey. It said, in the jargon of the time, 'Important. Anhealth, Surbiton, Telex. Suspected foot and mouth disease. Reginald Lumley, West Gill Farm, Aidensfield, near York. N.R. Police, Aidensfield.'

Having dispatched this, I next telephoned the local office of that organisation and asked for the Divisional Veterinary Inspector. The Ministry now had vets working all over the county but I asked them to send one to Reg's farm; I then called the County Medical Officer's department and notified them, after which I rang my own Force Headquarters and finally Sergeant Blaketon at Ashfordly.

He asked me what I'd done and I told him; I assured him I'd done everything necessary and that Reg was already providing disinfectant at his farm entrance. I explained that I was on my way to the farm within the next few minutes with my 'Keep Out' notices and to serve Form A upon poor old Reg to isolate his premises. I knew he would have quarantined his own farm, but the official wheels must turn.

I then put on my rubber leggings, a long waterproof mackintosh and Wellington boots. Dressed like this, I decided to walk the half-mile or so, for in this type of urgency we were no longer thinking in terms of minutes or seconds. Everything had come to a standstill and would remain so until the Ministry's vets had examined the suspect cow or cows. With my notices under my arm, and Reg's Form A in a buff envelope, I made my harrowing journey along the lane.

By the time I arrived at West Gill Farm, Reg was already in position at his gate. Dressed in oilskins and Wellington boots, he was standing guard with a shotgun in his hand. A large zinc bath full of pale yellow fluid stood just inside the gate. A yard brush lay beside it and a tractor and trailer were parked nearby.

"Now, Reg," I said.

"Noo then, Mr Rhea. Got all t' papers, hast tha?" His face was sad and drawn, and I knew I must be careful how I spoke to him. I must not be flippant at all, for farmers treat their cows like old friends. I knew he was on the verge of breaking into tears as he nodded towards the roll of notices under my arm.

"'Keep Out'" signs," I told him. "I'll stick 'em up for you, on all your entrances. This makes all entrances forbidden areas, Reg. This is the only one that leads down to the house and buildings, isn't it?"

"Aye, t'others are just gates into my fields."

"Good, well, I won't come through the gate. I'll do this job first — I've got some drawing-pins and string. I'll fix 'em on all the roadside trees and gateposts."

"Thanks. Ah've already had two daft townies trying to walk their dog down my road. Ah told 'em it was an infected spot, but they didn't understand. They reckoned it was a public footpath down to t' pond, so Ah said it was out o' bounds now and anyrood anybody coming in would have to paddle through that bath o' stuff. They didn't like that, nut wi' their townie shoes on. That's why Ah fetched my gun — folks don't argue wi' that, Mr Rhea. That lot sharp cleared off then an' Ah told 'em foot and mouth was catching for humans, an' all. It mebbe is, is it?"

"I'm not sure," I had to admit. "I know anthrax can be caught by people."

"Aye, well, it's matterless now. You go and stick them signs up and Ah'll stop folks tramping down my lane. You'll 'ave called in t' Ministry vets, have you?"

"I have, and they'll be here as soon as possible. It might be a while, they've other suspected outbreaks." I could see moisture in his eyes. His banter had concealed his genuine feelings, I felt, but now he would be alone once again with his thoughts. Before I left, I handed him his Form A, and then turned away to post the notices on his various entrances, eight in total. He was a sad and lonely figure as he waited with his gun in his hands, guarding his gate against ordinary people and a virulent disease. As I left, he opened my envelope, read the contents of the Form A and stuffed it into his pocket.

When I returned about forty minutes later, he was still there, pacing up and down as he looked out for the ominous approach of the vet's car.

"You go down to the house, Reg, I'll wait here," I offered.

"Nay, lad," he spoke softly. "Ah couldn't. T' wife and our lad are so upset . . . they'd only upset me. Ah'd allus be wanting to look in on me cows . . ."

"It's not confirmed," I tried to sound optimistic. "It could be a false alarm."

He shook his head. "Nay, Ah doubt it. It's all around is that disease; somehow, yan o' my cows 'as picked it up . . . it's t' end, Mr Rhea . . . t' end . . . twenty years work . . . all for nowt . . ."

"Don't upset yourself," I did not want to see this stalwart, tough farmer reduced to self-pity or tears, but he needed to talk to somebody. I happened to be that somebody; we were alone at the gate in our ungainly protective clothing, and we could look down the long straight track which led across his fields and into his compact clutch of farm buildings.

"Twenty years," he repeated, almost to himself. I looked at him. A sturdy Yorkshireman, turned fifty I guessed; he had the round, weathered face of his profession, a face which had seen little else but long hours and hard work over those years. But that work had produced some pride, too, family pride I guessed.

"Twenty years, it's takken me to build that herd. Pedigree Friesians, they are. Eighty milkers, Ah've got. Eighty and Ah started wi' nowt."

I glanced at the tall post which stood beside his main gate; it bore a small black and white sign which proclaimed that this was the home of the West Gill Farm Herd of Pedigree British Friesians.

"Ah did it for t' lad, for our Ted. Ah needed summat to pass on, Mr Rhea. He's grown up wi' them Friesians and knows 'em like they was bairns, Mr Rhea. We all do, every one on 'em. Me an' all, and t' wife. Seen 'em come along from calves, most of 'em. Bought some and bred some; fussed over 'em, made sure they were just right. Bedded 'em down at night, seen to 'em when they were badly . . . best Friesians for miles, they are."

He was staring into the distance as he talked, not looking at me and not looking down upon his farm in the shallow valley. He was gazing beyond all that, reminiscing and pouring out his heart in his own simple way.

"And now it's all gone . . . they'll be killed, all of 'em . . . put down like rats. Ah've been so careful, Mr Rhea, with foot and mouth about, taking care, watching where Ah bought things, where Ah went, disinfecting . . ."

"Don't," I said uselessly. "You're only making things worse. It might be a false alarm . . ."

I tried to give him a little hope.

"Nay, Ah knows foot and mouth when Ah sees it. Yon awd cow 'as it, there's nowt so sure . . ."

He went on to say how, as a young farmer, he had recognised the potential in a herd of Friesians; he'd seen them as ideal cattle for his plans, cattle which would produce first-class milk. They were useful beef animals too. So years ago, he decided to build himself a pedigree dairy herd, his own very special effort. And his idea was to introduce his only son, Ted, to the skills of dairy farming so that he, in turn, would continue with this herd. He wanted Ted to improve and expand it.

"Ah'd got all soorts of ideas in me head, Mr Rhea. Ah was gahin ti keep better records of 'em all, go for bigger milk yields an' that . . ."

It was good to hear him talking and I allowed him to ramble on, sometimes asking what I thought was a sensible question. I learned a good deal about Friesians that afternoon, but it also taught me enough about foot and mouth disease to make me realise the end had come. I didn't hold out much hope for his herd now, not after listening to his knowledgeable description of the disease and its drastic effects.

It would be over an hour later when a small car eased to a halt on the verge near the gate. A tall young man in a smart lovat-green suit climbed out and announced that he was Alan Porrit, a vet from the Ministry of Agriculture. After shaking hands and expressing his sorrow at the awful news, he announced his approval of our immediate actions and donned his own waterproofs.

After swilling himself in the disinfectant, he said, "Come along, Mr Lumley. Show me where to go."

"Nay," said Reg. "Ah can't. Ah just can't go down there. Not now . . . you go and get it ovvered with."

Tears welled in his eyes and he rubbed them roughly with his fist.

"Ah'm being right daft and sentimental, but you go. Ah can't . . ."

"I think you should, Reg," I said. "You'll be needed down there. I'll stay here."

After some gentle persuasion from us both, Reg joined the vet and I watched them walk into the distance. Their sorry figures seemed to diminish as they approached the farm, and then, as they reached the paths which divided one towards the byre and the other to the house, they halted.

From my vantage point on the lane, I could see them in deep conversation, then Reg began to shake his head. I saw him turn and walk towards his house. He left the vet standing alone. The vet turned on his heels and strode purposefully towards the byre which contained the suspect cattle.

As Reg approached the back door of his house, his hands were over his face. He was sobbing like a child. Someone inside opened the door; he went in and the door closed behind him.

That epidemic of foot and mouth disease cost the country over £200 million. No one knows how much it cost Reg Lumley.

CHAPTER 9

Is it, in heav'n, a crime to love too well?
ALEXANDER POPE, 1688—1744

In the great and pleasant rural landscape which surrounded Aidensfield during my time there, serious crime was practically unknown. Certainly, there were many minor thefts, most of which were never officially reported, and I'm sure there were motoring offences which never came to my notice. Other breaches of the law, such as drinking late in the country pubs or petty acts of damage or vandalism were dealt with in the spirit of the law rather than by the letter of the law. A quiet word in the right ear usually prevented further trouble.

It would be wrong to claim that Aidensfield and district was totally free from crime. It was not; every so often, an outbreak of criminal activity would occur, usually of the kind described as petty damage, theft or the unauthorised borrowing of cars. There were some housebreakings, shop-breakings and poaching, and if we suffered three crimes in the district during a month, the local papers described it as a crime wave.

These waves were very tiny, therefore, more like ripples on a village pond than the kind of waves that swamp ocean liners. Nonetheless, they did cause distress to the victims and this in turn caused anxiety among the villagers. From my point of view, these crimes, minor though they were, did involve my colleagues and me with extra duties. There were observations, report writing and court appearances, but I did not mind. In fact, I enjoyed the experiences they provided, albeit with deep concern for the victims, for the investigation of crime is fascinating. To investigate and detect crime is probably one of the major reasons for anyone joining the police service.

As time passed, and as each minor breach of the criminal law was dealt with, I did begin to wonder if a major crime or series of crimes would ever occur on my patch. I began to feel that this period of peace was too good to be true, and then, in the spring of one year, I was faced with an outbreak of arson.

Arson was, and still is, one of the most serious of crimes and the legal definition then said that arson involved the unlawful and malicious setting fire to buildings, including churches, warehouses, railway stations, shops and sheds, as well as crops, vegetable produce, coal-mines and ships. It was then categorised as a felony both at common law and by statute. The common law crime was confined to houses and their outhouses, while the statutory crime, featured in the Malicious Damage Act of 1861, involved a detailed list of the objects of the kind listed in the above definition. I remember that in those days, it was not legally possible to charge anyone with arson to a motor vehicle or television set because new-fangled contraptions of that sort were not mentioned in that 1861 Act — other possible charges such as malicious damage to personal property had to be considered.

In the weeks following that first act of arson there developed a series of troublesome fires, all of which involved either haystacks or hay in barns. I could discern no pattern, except that the attacked barns or stacks were usually in isolated locations. Some, however, were in the centre of our market towns and as time went by, I began to despair of ever catching the fire-raiser. Some of the fires were on my beat, and although all the local officers were involved in the investigation, I felt it was my duty to arrest the culprit. The battle both to halt and deal with the villain became a personal challenge.

News of the first fire came in the early hours of a Saturday morning in April. Just after 1 a.m. a passing motorist noticed flames licking the asbestos roof of a Dutch barn. He roused the farmer and his wife, who called the Fire Brigade by dialling 999. As a matter of routine, I was informed by our Control Room and clambered from my warm bed around quarter past one.

Rather than waste time climbing into my motorcycling outfit, I used my own car to rush to the fire. It was at Low Dale Farm, Briggsby, less than ten minutes' drive from Aidensfield. The farm, a small concern with livestock, poultry and arable land, was owned by Arthur Stead and his wife, Helen. When I arrived, the Fire Brigade was already there. Hoses were spraying hissing water into the fierce centre of the fire which had a very secure hold. Men were working in the heat of the flames as the bales of hay glowed in the night. The flames cast frightening shadows upon the house and nearby buildings and showered dangerous sparks across the dark countryside. Most of the flames licked the exterior surface of the hay, while a stiff night breeze carried sparks and more flames into the interior of the barn. Small new fires were breaking out all over the place; it looked like a lost battle.

With old raincoats over their nightclothes and Wellingtons on their feet, Arthur and Helen, both in their late fifties, were using hayforks in an attempt to pull untouched bales clear of the inferno.

Helpers had arrived from neighbouring farms and cottages. Men and women were working around the barn, removing bales by hand. After announcing my arrival to the Fire Brigade, I used the Steads' telephone to relay a situation report to Control Room, and then joined the rescue effort. I began to haul bales from the barn and throw them clear of the spreading blaze.

One problem lay in a stiff easterly breeze which made the hay glow deep within the stack as the intense heat consumed the dry material. We tried to hoist some burning bits well away from the barn, but the speed of the fire's consumption beat us. Gallons and gallons of water were sprayed into the depths and we did manage to remove a considerable amount of uncharred hay.

During a lull, I spoke to Arthur.

"We've got a fair amount out, Arthur," I commented, wiping my dirty hands across my face. We were all black from the smoke and sweating profusely in spite of the chill night air.

"T' cows won't eat it, Mr Rhea, even if it 'as been saved. It'll smell o' smoke, you see . . . might mak bedding or summat . . ."

"You'll be insured, are you?" I asked.

"Aye, but cows can't eat insurance money; they need fodder. It's a while yet before we can turn 'em out to fresh grass."

I knew that the local farmers would rally to help poor Arthur with his forthcoming feeding problems; they always did when anyone suffered a loss of this kind. But we had fought a losing battle. As fast as we removed bales, others burst into flames; it seemed as if the blaze had crept deep inside the stacked hay and I wondered if our removal of the bales loosened the packed hay and permitted the air to enter. This would fan the flames. As things were, it wasn't long before the entire contents of the barn were a mixture of searing heat, smoke and untidy charred hay.

We kept an eye on the drifting sparks but they disappeared across the fields and missed the buildings. As dawn came to Low Dale Farm we could see the full extent of the devastation. The barn was burnt to a shell, some roof portions having collapsed when the supports gave way in the fire. It contained a jumbled mass of charred and useless hay which was still smouldering. It would continue to smoulder and smoke for days. All around were piles of hay which had been saved by the volunteers, hay which the cattle would not now touch because it was tainted by smoke. The entire area was saturated with dirty water and we stood in a sea of mud and straggly strands of hay.

Arthur and Helen gave us all a breakfast of ham and eggs with copious quantities of hot tea. As we stood outside and I gathered the information necessary for my Fire Report, one of the senior fire officers took me to one side.

"Constable," he said, "we feel this is a suspicious fire. We can almost certainly rule out spontaneous combustion which, I'm sure you know, causes a good many stacks and barn fires. That usually occurs within three months of a stack being built — this one is eight months old. Fire from spontaneous combustion works from the inside and moves to the exterior. This started on the outside walls of hay, so it looks deliberate. The seat of the blaze was on the outside of the hay, at the east end of the barn, low down upon the stacked hay but just off ground level. There was a platform of hay left where some upper bales had been removed, and the blaze was creeping up the outside walls of hay when our men got here. I am confident that spontaneous combustion is not the cause and that an outside agent is responsible. It could be an accident, but I'm calling in our experts for their opinions."

This meant I must now inform the CID who would liaise with the Fire Brigade and a formal investigation would commence. It would be backed by statements from witnesses plus any scientific evidence salvaged from the scene. Inevitably, poor old Arthur and his wife would be under suspicion of having deliberately set fire to their hay for insurance purposes, and I knew the investigation had to be thorough, if only to exonerate them. I was sure they would never resort to this kind of evil. My witnesses were Arthur and Helen themselves, several fire officers and the motorist who had noticed the blaze, but none could provide any real evidence to show how the blaze had started. It remained a matter of opinion and speculation but continued to be 'suspicious'.

A week later, there was a second blaze. Although this one did not occur on my beat, it was only four miles away at Seavham and the circumstances were very similar. Around two o'clock in the morning, Ronald Thornton and his wife Alice, who farmed at Home Farm, were roused by barking dogs. Wary of intruders, they had peered out of their bedroom window to see one of their haystacks ablaze. It was in the corner of a field, away from the buildings, but was valuable for livestock feeding.

I noted the date and time, and although I did not attend this one I did later contact the Fire Brigade to ascertain whether it could be linked to the blaze at Low Dale Farm. Other than to say the cause was not spontaneous combustion, the Fire Brigade would not commit themselves. Nonetheless, the similarities included an isolated haystack, an outbreak in the early hours of a Saturday morning, and the suspicious nature of the blaze. The Thorntons were not insured, I learned, which somewhat added to the mystery.

If they had not done it deliberately which seemed most unlikely, and if it was not an accident (there were no chimneys or exposed flames nearby), and if it was not spontaneous combustion, then who had done it and why? These were the questions we had to answer.

I tried to find links or more similarities with the Stead fire but failed. My avenues of investigation included bad business deals; possible fraud; family feuds; jealousy, petty spitefulness or malice; the work of a pyromaniac and a host of other domestic and business likelihoods. To my knowledge, no known arsonist lived in the area.

The next blaze was three weeks later, on a Wednesday night at Crampton. It was discovered earlier than the others, around eleven o'clock. A neighbour had smelled smoke and had investigated the cause only to discover bales of hay well ablaze in the barn of Throstle Nest Farm. This barn was close to the centre of the village and, happily, there was no strong breeze to fan the flames or to disperse the dangerous sparks among the houses.

Mr and Mrs Bill Owens farmed Throstle Nest; their splendid farmhouse occupied an elevated site surrounded by its spacious land, and a pair of Dutch barns stood at the bottom of a lane. This lane formed a junction with the road which led into the village, and their neighbour, Jack Winfield, lived in a cottage near that junction.

Jack's swift action and the rapid response by the Fire Brigade kept damage to a minimum, but the familiar story emerged. It was another suspicious fire, so like the earlier ones. As the Brigade fought the fire and helpful villagers removed bales of unburnt hay, the drifting smoke penetrated many nearby homes. The smell would linger for days afterwards. During a lull, I spoke to Jack Winfield, a retired farm worker.

"Now, Jack, did you hear or see anything? We've had a few of these fires now."

"There was a motorbike about the village tonight," he said without hesitation. "I grumbled, 'cos it made my television picture go funny. Motorbikes do that, you know, sometimes."

"What time?" I asked.

"Nine o'clockish," he said. "First time, that was. Then again later, before t' fire broke out. Not long before, but I couldn't be sure of t' time really. Same bike, I could tell by t' noise."

"Has it been before?"

"Can't say I've noticed it. Mind, if I hadn't had my set on, mebbe I wouldn't have noticed."

"Did you see it then? Do you know who it was?"

"Sorry, lad, no."

After quizzing him at length, I took a written witness statement from him. For the first time, we had a hint of a suspect, slender though it was, and before the Fire Brigade left, one of their officers came to me.

"We found this," he said, opening the palm of his hand to reveal a spent match.

"Where, precisely?" I asked, accepting this new piece of evidence.

"About five feet from where we believe the blaze started," he said, pointing to a piece of muddy land. "We think it started low down this side, where some bales have been removed . . ."

"Like the Low Dale fire?" I interrupted.

"Yes, in a similar position. The flames crept up the outside wall of hay before gaining a strong hold. This match, which is clean and new as you can see, was lying on the ground."

"Thrown away, you think?"

"Its position suggests that."

I pinpointed the precise location of this match and drew a little sketch in my notebook so that it would be committed to paper for future records. It was an ordinary match, not from a book of paper matches or a short-stemmed Swan Vestas. Its unweathered appearance said a lot; there was a distinct possibility that it was associated with the blaze.

I reported these new facts to Sergeant Blaketon at Ashfordly, and he decided to institute a series of nightly police patrols. Their purpose was to trace the motorcyclist and/or the fire-raiser. At this stage, we felt there was little point stopping all motorcyclists but did decide to record the registration number of every bike seen during our patrols. I was aware, too, that the fuel tank of a motorcycle contains petrol and what better method is there for a fire-raiser to carry this incendiary aid?

If and when another fire broke out, we could consult our records and check the movements of all recorded bikes. It would be possible to see if they tallied with the date, time and place of the fire. Even so, with such a massive rural area to patrol, the chances of a police vehicle crossing the path of the fire-raiser were remote to say the least. But we had to try.

For the next couple of weeks there were no reported stack fires. We began to feel that our presence on the roads and the fact that our purpose was enhanced by local gossip, had deterred the arsonist. But we were wrong.

The next fire broke out in the centre of Ashfordly. Tucked into one of the side streets was a farmhouse and behind it was a square stackyard and a motley collection of implement sheds. The fields belonging to this farm were some distance away on the outskirts of the town, but this curious town centre farm, known as Town Farm, was a thriving enterprise.

I was on night duty one Friday and was patrolling the surrounding moors and hills when I spotted a bright blaze in the centre of Ashfordly. It was 1 a.m. For a moment, I thought it was a bonfire in a garden, one which had been lit earlier and whose flames had been revived by a sudden night breeze; but in seconds, I knew it was too large for that and I feared the worst.

From my vantage point on the hills, it was impossible to say precisely where it was. All I could determine was a bright, flickering flame somewhere among a dark collection of houses and other buildings. I accelerated the little motorbike down towards the town and it was then that I recalled the tumble of farm buildings and sheds just off Field Lane. As I entered the town, I knew the worst. I roared towards the blaze. It was now showing as a bright orange and red glow against the sky above the houses, and I could see a pall of thick, black smoke. This was no garden bonfire and I feared another arson attack.

The moment I turned the corner and identified the precise location, I halted and radioed my Control Room. Through its radio network, the Fire Brigade was summoned and I asked Control Room sergeant to awake Sergeant Blaketon. Then I began to rouse the sleeping occupants of the farmhouse and several nearby homes. The horrified farmer said there were horses in some of the buildings and so I helped him to evacuate his animals.

Two tractors were in the Dutch barn; they were already covered with blazing hay which had tumbled from the stacked bales and so began another battle to save his equipment and machinery. The farmer's wife was in tears; neighbours were terrified for their homes and the horses were snorting and frisky in their fright.

We did not save the barn, the hay or the tractors but no human or animal life was lost. With Sergeant Blaketon at my side, I began a meticulous search of the scene. We were seeking that spent match which could be some distance from the barn. He found it. Lying five or six feet away from where the wall of the hay had been, he located a clean spent match, miraculously having avoided the trampling feet and gallons of rushing water. He preserved it for evidence. It was another important indication that the same person was responsible for all the fires.

The Fire Officer in charge said he believed the blaze had not been due to an electrical fault or to spontaneous combustion; he expressed an opinion that the tractors might, in some way, have been responsible. The possibility of a short circuit from a battery couldn't be ignored.

A more detailed investigation would follow and the charred remains would be examined. When we told the firemen about the match, he said, "That figures. We think it might have started on that outer wall of hay, not far from there . . . that's the second match you've found, eh?"

We began to ask about the motorcycle noises in the night and one of the neighbours, a retired bank manager, did tell us he had heard a motorbike. It was not mine because the timing was different. I hadn't been near the place until just after 1 a.m. He had heard one about midnight, he said, but could not say whether it was coming towards Town Farm or leaving it.

But it was enough for us, after that, we intensified our nightly patrols for the motorcycling fire-raiser. At the same time, we renewed our enquiries from earlier victims. We asked them whether they had antagonised anyone who owned a motorbike and we continued our efforts to establish a link, any link, between all the scenes of the fires.

But we did not find any connection.

Then I had a stroke of luck. It was one of those moments of good fortune that all detectives require and with which some are blessed throughout their careers. In my case, it happened while I was off duty. I recognised the clue for what it was and became excited when I realised I might have found the arsonist.

It was a Friday, which was market day in Ashfordly. I went to market with Mary to help with the shopping and to look after the children. For me, it was a trying but enjoyable chore. I was wandering among the stalls in my off duty casual clothes, pleased that it was a fine spring day and that there were books and antiques to examine. I ran into friends and acquaintances to chat with and the entire experience generated a pleasing air of rustic contentment. It was a welcome break from my routine.

Then, as I poked among some junk on a stall, seeking old inkwells (which I collect as a hobby) I noticed the motorcyclist. He was sitting astride a green BSA Bantam in front of one of the pubs which overlooked the market-place. He was laughing and chatting to a pretty girl. I watched and, because motorcycles were very much on my official mind, began to observe them.

I was in an ideal position. As I watched, I saw the youth dig into his trousers pocket, pull out a cigarette and light it. Then, having done so, he flicked the spent match over his shoulder and drew heavily on the cigarette. My heart thumped; I found a pen in my pocket and jotted the make and registration number on a piece of paper and followed with a description of him and his girl. Then, I ambled across to find that match. I had to have it for comparison with the others.

It was easy; it was the only one lying nearby. The youth was engrossed in his chat with the girl and didn't even glance at my approach. The match lay about five feet behind him.

Not wishing to draw his attention, or indeed anyone else's, to my curious behaviour, I 'accidentally' dropped my car keys close to the match then stooped to retrieve them and my valuable piece of evidence. Now, the match would be scientifically compared with those already in our possession, and discreet enquiries would be made into the owner of that BSA. The chain of evidence was growing stronger. I went straight to Ashfordly Police Station with the match, and Sergeant Blaketon said he would have it taken immediately to the Forensic Laboratory at Harrogate.

Prompt enquiries from the Vehicle Taxation Office at Northallerton told us that the youth lived at Malton; we learned he was called Ian Clayton. And so, at last, we had a very likely suspect.

The problem was whether to interview him immediately, in which case he could deny being near the fires, or to make some discreet enquiries and observations with a view to gathering more evidence and facts about his life and background. We decided we needed more evidence if we were to link him with the fires; after all, we had no proof yet, merely surmise, and so we circulated to all police officers, his description and details of his motorcycle. We would find out about his work and how he spent his leisure hours and if necessary, his movements would be monitored as he went out at night. We might even catch him in the act of lighting a fire.

Two days later, we received a telephone call from the Forensic Science Lab at Harrogate. Their experts had examined all three matches and said that, in their opinion, they were similar.

Scientific evidence confirmed they had come from the same manufacturer and even the same batch of timber, but the lab experts would not commit themselves to anything more positive. A written report would follow. As evidence of arson, this was, in itself, far too flimsy. Our suspect remained a mere suspect.

Two weeks later, the little BSA Bantam was seen heading towards Ashfordly. It was discreetly followed and Ian Clayton collected his girlfriend from a house at 45 Stafford Road, Ashfordly. With each perched astride the tiny bike, it motored towards Waindale. It was about ten-thirty and it was dark. Having shadowed them into Waindale in his patrol car, PC Gregson radioed for me because Waindale was on my beat. He said they had driven along Green Lane. I received the call and set off for that hamlet. There was a feeling of excitement in my bones.

I used my own car because I felt this would be wiser than using the police motorcycle. A police motorcycle was far too prominent for this task. I parked in Waindale, making sure the car was out of sight, and began to walk along Green Lane, seeking haystacks and Dutch barns. I knew the location of most, and then, as I silently moved along the lane, I arrived at Green Farm. In the darkness, I could distinguish the tall supports of the Dutch barn, and then, as I padded silently into the complex, I came across the BSA Bantam. I could smell the heat of its engine as it leaned against a drystone wall, and a quick examination of its number plate proved it was the one we sought. My heart was thumping now; I had to find him before he fired this stack, but I also needed evidence of his crimes.

Other than the sounds of the night, including some furtive scuttlings from rats and mice, I could not see or hear anything. But he was here. Had he seen me? Was he watching me? If I wasn't careful, he might escape on his bike . . . perhaps I should have disconnected the plug lead?

All kinds of worries and plans crossed my mind, and then, as I stood in the shelter of a tractor shed, my eyes became accustomed to the gloom. Aided by a low light from the curtained farmhouse windows, I saw the flicker of a match. It burnt a hole in the gloom; it flickered for a few seconds and then flew in an arc to splutter into darkness. This was it!

I sped towards that place. The match had died now. It had not set fire to anything. But there was another tiny glow of red. And I smelt smoke. Cigarette smoke. Not burning hay.

I shone my torch. A pool of light burst upon the young couple, boy and girl, each partly dressed, each acutely embarrassed after their love-making in the hay. And in those moments, the youth's smouldering cigarette was cast away to land somewhere in the dry hay . . .

I found it before it ignited the hay, kept it as evidence and took them both to Ashfordly Police Station in my car. To cut a long story short, after a protracted investigation about their movements, Ian Clayton and Susan Longfield did admit visiting all the burnt barns and stacks. They identified them only when we took them to each one in turn. Susan, being new to the area, and Ian, living fifteen miles away, had seen the reports in the newspapers, but had never realised the fires had occurred in barns they had used. Names of villages and isolated farms meant nothing to them.

They had not known the names of the farms they had visited; they had simply jumped on the little bike and toured the lanes until they came to a warm and cosy barn or haystack. There they stopped and made love in the hay.

And afterwards, Ian always lit a cigarette which he discarded without thought . . .

He was charged with arson of each of those stacks and barns and appeared before the magistrates in committal proceedings. After considering all the facts, they found no case to answer because the fires were accidental. In their considered opinion, there was no malice in his actions and they accepted he had not unlawfully and maliciously set fire to the hay.

Another of my rare major criminal investigations concerned a case of housebreaking which even today remains unsolved.

Tucked discreetly behind the village street in Aidensfield is St Cuthbert's Cottage, a delightful small house which dates to the eighteenth century. With two bedrooms, a living-room and kitchen, it has beamed ceilings, pretty windows and roses growing around a rustic porch. When its elderly occupant died, it was bought by a Mr Lawrence Porteous of Leicester who wanted it as a holiday home. He retained most of the old lady's antique furniture, but modernized and decorated the little house until it was a veritable gem. It was the kind of home for which any romantic young couple would have yearned.

At this time, it so happened that one young couple from Aidensfield desperately needed a home. In their estimation, St Cuthbert's Cottage was ideal. They lacked the funds to buy it, but after the sale they did write to Mr Porteous to ask if he would rent them the cottage even for a short period, until they found somewhere of their own. He refused.

They wrote again a week or two later, pointing out that it was empty for most of the year, and that they had no home . . . but again he refused.

The situation had arisen like this. Jill Knight, nee Crane, was the youngest daughter of Mrs Brenda Crane, widow. Mrs Crane and Jill had lived in another Aidensfield cottage which was owned by a property company. When Jill married young Paul Knight, he moved into the same cottage and, with his new bride, shared the accommodation and its running expenses. Then Jill became pregnant. Through one of those awful quirks of fate, poor Mrs Crane suffered a heart attack and died about the same time.

The house had been in her name; consequently upon her death, the property company wanted to repossess it for another tenant, a retiring employee of theirs. Because Jill and Paul were not holders of the rent book, they were told to vacate the house. If they refused, then the due processes of civil law would be implemented to evict them. They were given three months' notice. This put them in a terrible dilemma. Paul worked for an agricultural implement dealer in Ashfordly and needed another home in the area, so that he was near enough to cycle to work. He couldn't afford a car and the buses were too infrequent.

Wisely, he applied for a council house but was told there was a waiting-list; his name would be placed on that list and in the meantime, he must find alternative accommodation. Not surprisingly, he got his eye on St Cuthbert's Cottage as an ideal short-term solution and that was how he came to write to Mr Porteous.

Repeated refusals from Lawrence Porteous put the youngsters in a real dilemma. I knew them both and liked them, but I could see the strain beginning to have its effect, especially upon the heavily pregnant Jill. The worry made her pale and constantly tired, and she began to neglect her appearance. Her mother's death, her own pregnancy and the housing problems were more than any young girl should have to tolerate.

"No luck?" I met her in the shop one day.

She shook her tousled head.

"Paul's been asking all over," she said, her pretty face drawn with anxiety. "We got chance of a council house over at Scalby, but it was too far for Paul to get to work. If you see anything, Mr Rhea, you'll let us know? They can't put us on the street, can they? Me being pregnant and that?"

"No, I'm sure they can't and I'm also sure something will turn up . . ."

"We only need something till we get a council house near here," she said. "There's bound to be one soon, isn't there? The council said they come up fairly often."

I did feel concerned for them. There were lots of suitable cottages in the surrounding villages, but this was the period when rich folks were buying them for holiday homes. Some were purchased as personal holiday homes or weekend cottages, and others were bought as investments to be rented weekly or for mere weekends to holiday-makers.

There is little doubt that the merits of this upsurge in buying country cottages did have a dual value; it did prevent many old cottages from falling into ruin and it did bring some welcome business into the village stores and inns. But on the other hand, it denied many young people a village home, either for rent or for purchase, because it made fewer local homes available.

This was brought home to me by the case of Jill and Paul Knight. I felt sure the council would never allow them to be thrown onto the street or taken into a hostel of some kind, but the wheels of official departments turn so very slowly and with such a lamentable lack of feeling or compassion. The officials would have no concept of the heartache involved in the long periods of waiting and hoping.

As I worried about the future for Jill and Paul, I received a visit from the postman.

"Mr Rhea," he said as he knocked with my morning mail, "somebody's broken into that little cottage down the village, St Cuthbert's."

My heart sank.

"Much gone?" I asked.

"Dunno," he shook his head. "They got in by smashing a window at the back, in the kitchen. It's still open."

"Right, thanks," I said. "I'll go and have a look."

As he'd said, entry was by smashing a pane at the back. The burglars, or housebreakers, had opened the kitchen window and climbed through. Once inside, exit had been through the kitchen door by unlocking the Yale catch. I could not tell whether anything was missing for I had never previously been in the cottage, and the intruder(s) had not made a mess.

I now had a crime in Aidensfield. If the breaking and entry had occurred after 9 p.m. and before 6 a.m. it would be classified as a burglary. Outside those times, it would be recorded as a housebreaking. Since 1968, due to a change in the law, all such breakings have been categorised as burglary.

I contacted the key-holder, Miss Cox, who lived two doors away and together we made a brief examination. I asked her not to touch anything, but to look around and tell me what was not in its usual place.

"Oh dear, oh dear," she muttered as she surveyed each room at my side. "Oh, dear, oh dear, how awful."

She was a fussy little woman of indeterminate age, probably in her sixties.

"Can you tell me what's been taken?" I asked, notebook at the ready.

"The television," she said, pointing to an empty corner.

I quizzed her and found out it was a black and white Murphy set, with a twelve-inch screen.

"The radio," she said in the kitchen. This was a Bush portable in a red and cream case, with a plastic carrying handle. "And a vase, a nice old vase in green glass."

"Thanks."

We searched the entire cottage, but nothing else seemed to have been stolen. She checked it regularly but could not say it was secure at 9 o'clock last night. So we recorded it as housebreaking, a lesser crime than burglary. I thanked her and obtained the telephone number of Mr Porteous; then called in our CID and Scenes of Crime experts; they would examine the cottage for fingerprints and other clues.

My next task, apart from completing the formal written Crime Report, was to make house-to-house enquiries around Aidensfield in the hope that someone had either heard or seen something. The CID would do their skilled work after obtaining a key from Miss Cox and I asked the local plumber to re-glaze the broken window.

From my office, I rang Mr Porteous to break the bad news. After assuring him that all possible had been done, and that his cottage would be secure before nightfall, he decided not to drive up from Leicester. I said it was not necessary.

Funnily enough, another two cottages in a deep moorland village were raided about a fortnight later, but in each case, the MO was different from the Aidensfield crime. I was sure the Aidensfield housebreaker had not broken into the others but those crimes did prompt a telephone call from Mr Porteous.

"Ah, Mr Rhea," he said. "I've just seen the paper — two cottages have been burgled on the moors. Is this a regular happening in your area?"

"It's becoming more commonplace," I had to admit. "Some of these holiday homes, with expensive furnishings, are easy meat, you know. They're empty for long periods and it doesn't take a genius to realise they've got things like TVs and radios inside; all easily disposable."

He paused. "We're going abroad for the summer," he said, "so we won't be using St Cuthbert's Cottage for our fortnight's holiday. It'll be empty from now until October; that's six months. Miss Cox will pop in from time to time, but you'll keep an eye on it for me, will you?"

"Of course," I said, "but it's always at risk, you know that."

"I know. I've heard about these people who live in houses for you, house-sitters or something. Have you anyone in your area who would do that? For a fee, of course."

I was about to say I knew of no one, when I remembered Jill and Paul Knight.

"I know a young couple who would do a good job for you," I said. "They'd be willing to house-sit for you, for six months or whatever it takes."

I told him all about Jill and Paul, and how they were now waiting for allocation of a council house. He recalled their pleading letters.

"I didn't commit myself before," he said. "After all, I don't know them and at that time I did intend using my cottage most weekends . . . but, well, for a gap of six months . . ."

"They are on the council waiting-list," I stressed, "but this would be useful to both you and them."

"Ask them to ring me," he said, "I'll discuss terms; I was willing to pay someone, so I may decide to allow them the cottage rent free or possibly a nominal rent, for legal purposes . . ."

Three days later, they moved in.

Five days afterwards, the stolen goods were found in an old van which was rotting in a quarry. They were quite undamaged and after successfully testing them for finger-prints, they were restored to St Cuthbert's Cottage. It was good news for Mr Porteous.

My enquiries into the crime drew a complete blank but it was a remark I overheard from a drinker in the Brewers Arms which caused me to think.

"By gum," said the man over his pint one night, (he was chatting confidentially to a pal, but I heard him), "it's a rum sort of a do when you've got to burgle a house to get folks to take notice of you. Still, yon lad's got a roof over his head now."

From time to time, I still reflect upon that unsolved crime.

THE END

ALSO BY NICHOLAS RHEA

COMING SOON

Gorgeous new Kindle editions of the **Constable Nick** books soon to be released by Joffe Books. Don't miss a book in the series — join our mailing list:

www.joffebooks.com

FREE KINDLE BOOKS

Do you love mysteries, historical fiction and romance? Join 1,000s of readers enjoying great books through our mailing list. You'll get new releases and great deals every week from one of the UK's leading independent publishers.

Join today, and you'll get your first bargain book this month!

Follow us on Facebook, Twitter and Instagram @joffebooks

DO YOU LOVE FREE AND BARGAIN BOOKS?

Thank you for reading this book. If you enjoyed it please leave feedback on Amazon or Goodreads, and if there is anything we missed or you have a question about, then please get in touch. The author and publishing team appreciate your feedback and time reading this book.

We're very grateful to eagle-eyed readers who take the time to contact us. Please send any errors you find to corrections@joffebooks.com

Printed in Great Britain
by Amazon